THE HEARTWOOD WEDDING

A HEARTWOOD SISTERS NOVEL (CARTER'S COVE BOOK 4)

ELANA JOHNSON

AEJ
CREATIVE WORKS

ISBN-13: 978-1-953506-27-6

1

Bradley Keith positioned the hardhat on his head, the construction site before him like a breath of fresh air. He loved the scent of concrete dust combined with the salty air only found on the island of Carter's Cove.

He'd been back in town for a few years now, and gratitude for this hometown project spread through him. Sometimes his jobs took him all over the South, and it was nice to have a construction site just down the road from where he lived.

The Heartwood Inn was the premier destination on the island, and they wanted another pool on the second floor for their VIP guests.

The floor was relatively quiet, as most of their conference center space sat on this floor, along with two huge ballrooms where the rich and famous booked their weddings. Brad knew, because his once-fiancée had booked their marriage-to-be right here at the inn. Thankfully, Emily had called off the wedding before Brad had had to do it.

"Where are we with the tiles?" he asked his floor supervisor.

James sighed. "They're delayed out of Atlanta. Apparently they've had some thunderstorms down there."

"Surprise, surprise," Brad muttered. He hated Atlanta, though he'd lived there for a few years. Started his construction business there, too. Maybe that was why he held such antagonistic feelings toward the city.

Because he'd almost lost everything there too, thanks to another fiancée that hadn't become his wife. And he had been the one to tell Tamara that the relationship wasn't going to work out between them.

That single act had caused him to lose his biggest financial backer—Tamara's father.

He wiped the memories from his mind as he surveyed what looked like one big hole in the cement. "Is she cured?"

"Yep," James said. "We just need those tiles. I have the guys working on the floor today. That'll be the second coat. We'll do the walls while we wait. And the floor tiles are in."

"They are? Show me those." Brad glanced at his clipboard as he followed James through the construction site.

A couple of men worked in the dressing rooms too, where the white subway tiles had gone in last week.

Brad felt like his whole life had been consumed by tiles. But when building an indoor swimming pool, that was kind of how things went.

"How was your date the other night?" James asked, stepping past a workbench filled with power tools.

"Oh, uh." Brad heaved another sigh. "I don't think I'm going to be seeing Carmen again." Anyone for that matter, but especially Carmen. He didn't date journalists, for one, and if he'd known who she was, he never would've agreed to go out with her. Number two, she hadn't really seemed interested in him, but in getting a story on him. And number three, she had the power to reduce him to ashes with a few strokes on her keyboard.

No, thank you. He'd left that high-profile life—but he hadn't been able to get out of the restaurant without a reason why he couldn't date her. He squirmed in his own skin just thinking about what he'd told her to get out of going on a second date with her.

"Why not?"

"I'm just not into the dating scene here," he said. "I grew up here, you know?"

"So? What does that have to do with anything?" James stopped in front of a stack of boxes. "These are the floor tiles for the pool surround."

Brad proceeded to cut through the tape on the top box to reveal—"These are red," he said.

"No." James frowned. "Didn't we order gray?"

"We sure did." Brad pulled one of the twelve-inch square tiles out of the box. "This is definitely red." He lifted the burnt orange tile almost above his head, wanting to smash it at his feet.

James made a sound like a leaking balloon, and he pulled his phone out of his back pocket. "I'll call them. Do you have the form?"

Brad did...somewhere. He looked at his clipboard and started flipping the papers attached there. "What was the name of the company again?" The letters in front of him blurred and rearranged themselves into nonsensical formations.

"Castle-something," James said.

A big C caught his attention, and he pulled that paper out of the top clasp. "I think this is it." No one knew about his reading struggles, and he'd managed to restart his business without help from anyone. Spending seventeen years playing professional football had allowed him certain...luxuries.

He'd returned to Carter's Cove, as there always seemed to be some sort of development going on here, and he'd managed to make a decent living the past few years.

"So you don't want to go out with Kelly," James said, looking at the paper.

"No," Brad said. "I'm not going out with anyone anymore." He'd been engaged twice, and he was thinking maybe he'd just stay married to his business, the way Tamara had claimed he already was.

Plus, at age forty-seven, he wasn't exactly in the prime years of his life for swimming in the dating pool. James had been the one to set him up with Emily here on the island, and in fact, every date Brad had been on once he'd re-established himself her in Carter's Cove had been set up by James.

"You could be missing out," James said, turning away a moment later with, "Yes, this is James Long with Keith Construction. We ordered...." His voice faded out, and Brad let him go.

He wandered out of the dressing room and back into the main pool area, where a few other people worked. He didn't have a huge construction firm, but he knew plenty of people, and when he got hired on a big job, he could bring the manpower.

He loved the beach, but he had a sudden longing to travel to Lexington, where he'd spent summers growing up on his grandfather's horse farm.

He'd lived a good life for his forty-seven years, even if he didn't have a wife and kids to show for it.

You might be missing out rang in his ears, but he scoffed them away. James didn't know what he was talking about. He couldn't even set Brad up with someone even remotely compatible with him, and they'd been friends for five years.

A feminine form moved past the plastic separating the

construction site from the rest of the hotel, and Brad turned away from the woman. Instant heat shot to his face, reminding him that even forty-seven-year-olds had hormones.

But Celeste Heartwood was one thousand percent off-limits. Not only was she completely out of his league, what with her pencil skirts and professionally pressed blouses—and those heels. Wow, Brad liked those heels that woman wore—but she knew she was out of his league.

"Did you hear me?"

"What?" Brad spun away from the plastic, where Celeste had been. She wasn't even there anymore, and foolishness hit Brad right between his ribs.

"They're putting a rush on the right tile," James said. "It should be here by the end of the week."

"Great," Brad said. "Great." He took a deep breath, wondering where he'd been on his to-do list for that morning before thoughts of Celeste had distracted him.

"Are you going down to South Port today?" James asked.

"Yes," Brad said, seizing onto the topic. "I do need to go down there."

"Okay, so—" He cut off so suddenly that Brad looked at him only to find him staring at something straight ahead. He followed his gaze to see Carmen Lunt standing there.

His stomach dropped to his boots, and whatever James

said didn't register in Brad's ears. All he could see was that fiery Latina stalking toward him. She said something in rapid Spanish that Brad knew enough to translate into something bad, and then she arrived in front of him.

"You said you were engaged?" The words echoed throughout the entire construction site, as it was mostly cement and very open.

"You said what?" James asked.

"I am," Brad said, his voice a little weaker than he'd like it to be.

"To who?" Carmen folded her arms and cocked one hip. Her head bobbled like one of those dolls, daring him to lie to her again.

He could see the headlines now.... He felt like he was falling for a moment, and his own name left his mind. Celeste walked by the plastic again, causing it to flutter, and he seized onto the idea. "Celeste Heartwood," he said. "There she is. Excuse me." He ducked around Carmen and jogged toward the plastic.

He'd known Celeste's family growing up, though he was quite a bit older than the woman herself. Olympia, her older sister, was probably five years younger than him, and Brad had competed in the surfing championship right here at the inn before he'd been drafted into professional football and shipped all over the country.

He'd spent the most time down in Florida, playing for the Falcons, where he'd ended his career after eight years there.

"Celeste," he called after her once he'd freed himself from the construction site. She turned back, surprise in those gorgeous eyes as she paused right outside her office door.

Gorgeous eyes? Where had that come from?

"Hey." He chuckled as he jogged up to her. "Can I talk to you? For a minute?" He glanced over his shoulder and back toward the construction site. James and Carmen hadn't emerged yet. She was his next-door neighbor, so maybe he was trying to calm her down.

Brad could hope and pray, and he needed a solution —fast.

"I suppose," Celeste said, confusion on her face.

"Great." He reached past her and twisted her door-knob, pushing the door in so she'd enter. Another quick look over his shoulder told him that he had maybe thirty seconds inside this office, as Carmen stood there, watching them now.

Celeste either didn't care or didn't see her, because she entered her office, one hand on the door while he followed. She closed the door and asked, "What's going on? Is there a problem with the construction? I can get the manager—"

"There's no problem with the construction." Brad pulled himself out of the situation and put himself on the football field. Sure, he'd retired from the league eight years ago, but he'd never focused better than when playing football.

And he needed to focus now, on the right things. Not Celeste's very feminine form, with all these curves and swells in the right place. Not her very pink lips that called to his male side. Not the pale blue eyes and the softly curled blonde hair that begged him to run his hands through it moments before he kissed her so completely that he'd forget the look of disdain on her face.

He really needed to get control of his thoughts, because he would never be with this woman.

"I said," she said. "What's the problem?"

"Oh, uh." He glanced behind him. "I need a favor, and I'm afraid I need it right now."

Carmen knocked on the door, a string of muffled Spanish following.

"What in the world?" Celeste asked, stepping one of those deliciously heeled feet toward the door.

Brad jumped in front of her. "I need you to say you're my fiancée."

Her eyes flew to his, wide and scared. Scared? Was that right?

Alarmed, for sure. Surprised. And yes, a little scared.

"Just tell her," he said. "Please, Celeste. It'll just be for the next ten minutes, and I just—" His voice got covered by louder knocking.

Pure desperation pulled through him, and he had no idea what he'd do if she said no.

She jumped as the door rattled in the frame as Carmen beat on it. She looked from it to him and tugged on the bottom of her blouse. It was pure white, with tiny pink palm trees on it, and Brad had a brief flash of the two of them lying on the sand, under some palm trees together.

"I'll take care of this," Celeste said, reaching for the door handle.

But that hadn't exactly answered Brad's plea, and he had no idea what she was going to say to the very angry woman on the other side of the door.

2

Celeste Heartwood had dealt with many dissatisfied customers over the years. Heck, she could weather a bridezilla in the worst of times, so the scowling woman standing in the hall didn't even scare her.

Oh, no, that honor belonged to the tall, beautiful man standing half a step behind her.

Bradley Keith, starting tight end for the Florida Falcons until a few years ago. Five, six, Celeste wasn't sure. She didn't really follow football, but he was the home-town hero, and she was well-connected around the island, so she couldn't avoid every bit of gossip about the man.

When she'd learned it was his construction firm heading up the pool project, she'd been glad for the piece of plastic that kept his powerful presence contained. He'd never been interested in much to do with Carter's Cove, and the proposal she'd put in to his construction firm for an outdoor wedding hall at the inn had gone unanswered.

Unanswered, as if the man didn't have time for anyone on the island where he'd grown up. Why he'd come back was a complete mystery to her.

"Can I help you?" she asked Carmen Lunt, who'd folded her arms.

"Are you engaged to this man?" she demanded.

The last man Celeste had been out with had once been her boyfriend, and she'd hated every minute of it. She didn't want to keep recycling through her past failures with men, but no one new had come asking for a while. Celeste had certain functions she had to attend for her job, and she couldn't show up without someone on her arm.

So Boyd and Andre had satisfied those requirements, but little else, and she'd sworn to Gwen she wouldn't go out with one of them again.

But maybe Bradley....

No, not Bradley, she thought, because he probably answered texts the way he answered business proposals— not at all, and she didn't need to go through that.

But she knew who Carmen Lunt was—and she would publish something terrible and completely untrue about Bradley in her lame society rag.

"Yes," she said, stepping back and linking her arm through his. "Do you have a problem with that?" Maybe she'd done it because she didn't like the look on Carmen's face. Maybe she could have Bradley for a few weeks. Maybe she just didn't want Carmen to get the gossip. Or maybe she'd gone insane.

The fire inside Carmen deflated quickly, until the moment turned awkward with the three of them standing there, facing off. She finally looked at Bradley, hissed something in Spanish, and stalked away.

Celeste fell back a step, bumping right into the very solid form of Bradley a bit behind her. "Sorry," she said, heat filling her whole body.

He moved away from her, collapsing into one of the chairs opposite of her desk. "I'm the one who's sorry, Celeste. Do you even know my name?"

"Of course I do," she said, practically scoffing the words. "You're Bradley Keith, the famous football star from Carter's Cove." She moved around her desk and sat down, her eyes glued to him.

He wore a hardhat that he took off to reveal a mop of dark hair. A beachy breeze could easily tousle that up so that she would have to run her fingers through it and straighten it all out again. Her hands twitched like she'd actually get to do that, and she knew in that moment that she'd truly gone mad.

"So we're engaged?" she asked when he said nothing.

He watched her with those bright blue eyes, though, almost seeing right through her carefully crafted façade.

All the jewelry. All the makeup. All the professional clothes, and the carefully curled hair.

Celeste loved putting all the pieces of herself together to make the very best picture she could. She loved putting forth a good impression, and she liked having people look at her like she had everything figured out.

And when it came to running the events and weddings at The Heartwood Inn, she did. But in her personal life? Celeste felt like a bomb had gone off, and she wasn't sure where all the pieces of herself had gone.

"Do you speak, Bradley?"

"Yes." He coughed and sat up straighter. "And it's just Brad. Only my mother calls me Bradley."

"Oh, I've heard your father talk about you, too," she said, fully flirting with him now and wondering when the real Celeste Heartwood would come back. "And I'm pretty sure he called you Bradley as well."

Brad brought out his smile, and Celeste was glad she could get him to do that. She could tame anyone, even the talented football star. "Yeah, okay. But they're the only ones."

"All right." She shuffled some perfect paperwork on her desk. "Brad. We're engaged?"

"Yeah, I just...I went out with her a few days ago, and it was not going well. So I told her I was engaged, and I kind of...left her in the restaurant." He cleared his throat and shifted in his seat. "Tried to play it off as a big misunderstanding."

"Oh-ho, I think she definitely got the understanding."

Brad chuckled and nodded. "You were quite convincing."

"I sounded a little catty, didn't I?" Celeste couldn't help laughing too, but she quickly covered her mouth, feeling self-conscious in this man's presence. Plus, she couldn't believe he'd make up such a story just to get out of a date. He must not have had too much experience if he had to resort to such things.

"Nah," he said, though she definitely had sounded a little catty. "Anyway, thank you. I'm in the clear now." He started to stand, a groan pulling through his throat.

Celeste stood up too, alarmed that he was leaving. For a reason she couldn't name, she didn't want this to be over. After all, what other reason would he have to jog toward her and bring all that delicious-smelling cologne into her office?

"I don't think you understand women," she said.

Brad's gaze flew to hers, clearly horrified. Or something along those lines. "I'm sure I don't."

"Carmen isn't just going to accept that and move on," she said. "In addition to her journalism—and I use that term lightly—she works at the salon, and that means she has a network of women she can ask about you."

His mouth opened, but he said nothing. He ran his hand through his hair and sighed. "So what do we do?" he finally asked.

"Well, you can start by finding me a ring to wear," she

said. "That way, the rumor will be perpetuated." Her thoughts flew to her sisters. They'd know within a matter of days, and then her phone would blow up. Gwen would stand in the bathroom door while Celeste brushed her teeth, and fire questions at her until Celeste wanted to gouge out her eardrums.

So she'd have a precious few days to keep this secret to herself.

"So wait," he said, standing up fully. "You're saying we need to *stay* engaged?"

"Yes," she said.

"For how long?"

"I don't know. What's a reasonable amount of time to be engaged? This was *quite* sudden."

Brad smiled again, and Celeste's flirting skills had rewarded her yet again. "I was once engaged for only six weeks," he said.

Celeste's eyebrows shot up. "You were?"

"Once," he said evasively, ducking his head. He was absolutely *adorable*, and Celeste couldn't believe she thought so. He was so different from the interviews she'd seen and the stories she'd read. So, so different.

"So let's start with six weeks," she said. "Can you take me to dinner tonight?"

"Tonight?" His voice broke, and he cleared his throat again.

All at once, Celeste realized he was nervous. This

incredibly handsome, strong, striking, ex-professional football player was *nervous* around *her*.

The sky had definitely fallen.

"I like Radish," she said, opening the door and standing beside it. "I don't get off until six though."

"Should I...pick you up here, or at your place?"

She held out her palm, feeling reckless and absolutely like lightning had struck her. "I'll put my number in your phone. You text me, and I'll send you my address."

Brad smoothly reached into his pocket and withdrew his phone. Celeste had never been happier that she kept her nails short as she tapped her number into his phone. "There you go, Bradley."

He took his phone and paused right in front of her, both of them crowded in the doorway. "It's just Brad, Celeste. I mean, I don't want to be reminded of my mother when we're...together." He reached up and tucked her hair behind her ear, sending fire though her whole body.

"Okay, I'll text you," he said, walking away.

Celeste leaned against the doorframe and watched him until he ducked back through the plastic barrier and into the new construction for the VIP pool. Her phone didn't chime right away, and that only made her heart beat a little faster than it already was.

She fanned herself as she backed into her office and closed the door, the realization of what she'd just done striking her in the chest.

"But maybe now you can move past Ben. And Boyd.

And Andre," she said aloud to herself, glad her assistant hadn't come in yet. She dove for her phone, because she couldn't go on a date with Brad without perfectly sculpted eyebrows.

THAT AFTERNOON, CELESTE RUSHED THROUGH THE LAST OF her prep for a four o'clock meeting with one of her December brides. Her appointment had taken a little longer than normal, as there had been a group of women who'd gotten there just ahead of her.

Didn't matter. She'd been through these files before, and she almost had them memorized. But she prided herself on being ultra-prepared with everything she needed to provide the ultimate experience for her brides.

"Leslie is here." Paige's voice chirped over the intercom in Celeste's office, and she closed her folders and reached for the button.

"I'm ready," she said, standing. She straightened her clothes and stepped over to the door. Paige opened the door and Leslie smiled at her as she walked in. "Thanks, Paige."

"Of course," she said. "Oh, and a very handsome man stopped by a few minute ago. He said he texted you and hasn't heard back." Paige's eyebrows went up as her lips curved.

"He did? Why didn't you send him back?"

"You said no distractions," Paige said, flipping her dark hair over her shoulder.

Celeste had said that, and there were no exceptions. As she closed the door and faced Leslie, she thought she should maybe put Brad on the exception list, if only because that was what she'd do for a real fiancé.

"Leslie," she said, pushing Brad out of her mind. "How are you?" She hugged her bride. "How's Rick?"

"He's great," she said. "The wedding is still on." She laughed lightly, and Celeste joined her though her laughter was a bit forced.

"I'm so glad," she said. "We have three things to decide today." And Leslie wasn't known for making quick decisions. "Let's start with the easiest one. The cake." She crossed to the table in her office, where Teagan had set up the three choices for Leslie's wedding.

"This one is our house-made carrot cake," she said. "It's delicious, and moist, and it has cream cheese frosting with chopped walnuts on top." She handed Leslie a tasting fork and continued with, "It's our largest cake, as you can see."

"Very robust," Leslie agreed, dipping her fork into the frosting and cake. She took a delicate bite, because everything Leslie did was dainty. "Mm, this is good."

"Classic chocolate," Celeste said, her stomach growling at her for skipping lunch. But she hadn't had time, and she never ate before going out with a new man.

That way, she'd be plenty hungry, and she wouldn't be self-conscious about eating in front of him.

Bradley Keith.

She could hardly believe he'd come into her office that morning. He clearly had no idea she'd submitted a proposal for his grant money, and she wasn't sure if that stung more or made the situation more tolerable.

"It has a rich chocolate ganache," she said, focusing on the cake. "As well as chocolate chips inside the cake."

"Wow, death by chocolate," Leslie said, barely taking enough to taste it.

"And our classic vanilla. The cream is lemon, with a very vanilla bean frosting."

Leslie took a bite of that one, and then another, and Celeste knew she'd found her winner. "Vanilla," she said.

"Great." Celeste crossed back to her desk. "I'll put it on the menu. Which leads us to the wine you want for the pre-dinner mingle." She indicated the row of bottles on her desk, which the inn's new wine connoisseur had selected specifically based on Leslie's questionnaire.

By the time she finished with Leslie, it was five-thirty, and she hadn't had a spare moment to text Brad. She picked up her phone, which had been on silent for hours, and saw he'd texted a while ago.

Her heart skipped a beat, and her fingers flew across the screen as she hurried to text him her address. *Say, seven?* she asked. *I'm still at work, and I want to change.*

He didn't answer immediately, and Celeste did something she hadn't done in a long time—she left work early.

Even Paige looked at her in surprise and asked, "Where are you going?"

Celeste turned and walked backward out of the office. "I have a date. Let's lunch tomorrow."

"I'm ordering now!" Paige yelled after her, and Celeste giggled as she walked down the hall, her heels practically clicking against the industrial carpet up here.

She pushed the elevator button, a giddy feeling prancing through her she hadn't felt in a long time. And probably shouldn't be feeling now.

Gwen worked an early shift in the inn's kitchens, as she managed all the food coming in or going out of the inn, including what they needed for the bakery, the on-site restaurant, room service, and on-beach dining.

It was a huge job, and she often left the house where she and Celeste lived by five o'clock in the morning. Celeste had a much more normal job, at least according to the hours she worked. She'd likely find Gwen sitting on the back porch, a paper plate with the remains of her dinner beside her, and a soft snore coming out of her mouth.

Celeste could change into something a little less professional, put on more lip gloss, and sneak out of the house in a pair of sandals so she could have an amazing first date with Bradley Keith.

Bradley Keith.

She grinned as she got on the elevator, more excited about this date than any she'd had in a long, long time.

So he'd snubbed her once. So had her other boyfriends, and she'd gone out with them again. She'd just see if the spark that had leapt between them in her office grew into a flame. That was all.

3

Annoyance sang through Brad when he got Celeste's text. No, he hadn't hurried right back to the construction site and messaged her immediately. But surely someone like her was attached to her phone at the hip, and she couldn't answer him for hours?

He'd even stopped by her office in an attempt to get an answer.

"Stupid," he muttered to himself. He'd probably come off looking like a fool, desperate for the Queen Bee to pay attention to him.

Still, at six-forty-five, he found himself swiping the keys to his convertible from the hook beside the garage exit and heading to the address she'd finally given him.

The house he pulled up to looked...quaint. That was how his mother would've described it. Cute, and quaint, and the perfect place to waste an afternoon on the beach.

Or whole days. The front yard was neatly trimmed, and the white siding gleamed in the evening sunlight. The sound of the ocean could be heard as he walked up the sidewalk, and he reminded himself that the Heartwoods had some serious money.

You do too, he told himself as he rang the doorbell and tucked his hands in his pockets. He'd done exactly what she'd told him to and spent part of the afternoon at the jewelry shop, getting a ring for his "fiancée."

When she finally opened the door, Brad drank in the sight of her. She was beautiful, and she possessed a sense of style that the socialites did in New York City. He'd played there for one year, and he generally wanted to wipe those twelve months of memories from his mind.

"Hey, Princess," he said, because that was what she was. "You look great." He could compliment her even if this whole thing was fake.

Her blue eyes sparkled, and for the first time, Brad thought she might not be looking down on him. "Thank you," she said. "You don't look so bad yourself."

He glanced down so he could remember what he wore. Blue jeans. Blue button-up. He looked into her eyes. "Thanks. So Radish? Isn't that some sort of, I don't know, fancy sushi place?"

"It's way more than sushi," she said. "They have steaks too. Lobster. Everything is divine."

Divine.

Brad almost started laughing, because he literally

didn't know a single person who talked like that. Oh, wait. Yes, he did. Celeste Heartwood.

"I'll take your word for it," he said, smiling at her. She wore a different pair of dangly earrings this evening, with a pair of skintight jeans and a bright yellow blouse covered in flowers. She wore sandals instead of heels, and Brad decided on the spot that he liked them as much as the fancier footwear she usually wore.

"We can go somewhere else, if you'd like," she said, though it was clear she did not want to dine somewhere else.

"Do you go out much, Celeste?" he asked, stepping back and turning to go down the steps.

"I don't see how that's your business."

"Well, seeing as how you're my fiancée, I think I should know quite a few things about you I don't yet know." Brad could sound dignified if he had to. When he'd played for the Falcons, he'd had a press secretary and a public relations director, who helped him—and all the players—put forth their best foot.

She joined him at the bottom of the steps and appraised him with the same coolness he'd always seen from her. Just once, he'd like to see her get ruffled. Lose an earring. Break a heel. Something.

"I suppose you're right," she said. "I go out a normal amount."

"Then you'd know that it's a *terribly* busy time on the island, and all the restaurants are full almost all the time."

"Oh, of course."

"So we'll go to Radish, because I got a reservation there, and they're expecting us."

"You got a reservation? When?"

"This morning, when you said I needed to take you to Radish." He cut a look at her out of the corner of his eye and kept walking down the sidewalk. "You did say six, but I called and got it moved back. We do need to get going, though." He opened the passenger door for her, but she just looked at the car.

"Worried about messing up your hair?" he asked. Celeste didn't seem like the type to enjoy driving down the coastal highway, the top down, her hair flying wildly behind her as the wind tried to steal it from her head.

"Yes," she said, giving him a hard glare. "A little, actually." She reached up and smoothed her perfect curls. "I spend a lot of time on my hair."

"It's beautiful," he said, wondering where the words had come from and if he really meant them. Of course he did. Celeste *was* a beautiful woman. Devastatingly beautiful, and his heart skipped a beat, then two.

She ducked her head and smiled, finally stepping past him and lowering herself into the car. He closed the door behind her and went around the back of the car, wondering why this felt like a real date.

He pulled open the door, the corner of it catching against his shin. He yelped and hopped back, cursing inside his head.

"Are you okay?" Celeste asked. "What happened?"

He wasn't going to tell her that he'd maimed himself with his own car door, as if he'd never gotten in a car before. "Nothing," he said quickly, his throat tight. He slid into the seat and started the car, flashing her a quick smile that didn't sit right on his face.

The music came on too loud, and his pulse sped as he hurried to turn it down. "Sorry." A nervous laugh accompanied the word, and Celeste gave him a tight smile. His mind spun as he drove, trying to find something to say to her.

"What are you working on right now?" he asked.

"At the inn?"

"Yeah," he said. "You do events there, right?"

"That's right," she said. "It's wedding season, so we're dealing with a lot of those, and of course, I'm dealing with my fall brides as well, and when I have time, I'm already booking for Christmas."

"Wow," he said, though he had no idea what it took to deal with a bride. "And I'm just trying to get the right tile in."

"How's the pool coming?"

"It'll get done," Brad said, because it would. "We're a bit behind schedule, but I've learned that being behind is the name of the game when it comes to construction."

"Isn't it?" she asked. "Why is that? Gwen and I had our bathroom remodeled, and it took two months to get the mirror in. The first time, it wasn't cut right, and it took ages to get it redone."

"Oh, those glass guys," he said. "They're the worst. And the thing is, once you find a good one, you can't leave them. They do such great work. And it's so specialized." Brad took a deep breath, because he realized what a boring topic of conversation this was.

"How'd you go from football player to construction manager?" she asked.

"I own the company," he said, a hint of pride in his voice he didn't mean to have. But it was there, nonetheless, and by the look on Celeste's face, she'd heard it.

"I'm aware," she said coolly.

Brad pulled into the parking lot at Radish and found a spot near the back. "What does that mean?"

"Nothing," she said, her voice too high and too airy. So it meant something. He studied her for another moment, but she turned away from him and got out of the car.

Brad went with her and into the ritzy restaurant, with all of its dim lighting and huge live lobster tank right by the hostess station. He found it insufferable, but he hoped the food would be good.

Problem was, at least a dozen people milled between the door and the hostess station, and Brad didn't want to just shove his way through. He could—he'd been trained to get through angry people trying to put him flat on his back—but he didn't want to.

He became aware of several people looking at him, and one man stepped right up to him. "Brad Keith, right?"

"That's right," he said with a smile. "Excuse me." He did position himself through the crowd, leaving Celeste somewhere in the fray behind him. This restaurant was his idea of a nightmare, and he'd much rather drive through a burger joint and find a bench at South Port to eat than stay here for another minute.

"Do you have a reservation?" the woman at the hostess stand asked.

"Yes," he said. "Brad Keith. It was at six, but I called and moved it to seven."

She looked down at her paper, which was filled with names and numbers and squares, all of it nothing but nonsense to Brad. "Your reservation was at six."

"I know," he said. "I just said that. But I called and moved it to seven."

"I...don't see that here." She looked up at him as if he could decipher her number system.

"Bradley Keith," he said again. "I called just over an hour ago."

"Let me ask Marcus." She turned toward another man, who stepped over and started studying the chart on the podium.

"I'm so sorry, sir," he said. "We don't have any other tables, and we weren't able to change your reservation from six to seven."

Frustration built within him. "That's not what the woman said when I called."

"When did you call?" Marcus asked.

Brad could see this was a fight he wasn't going to win. "Never mind. Thank you so much." He turned away from the hostess station as Marcus started to say something else. Suddenly, all of the eyes on him felt twice as heavy, and he shouldered his way back to where Celeste stood.

"Bad news," he said, leaning closer to her ear. The scent of roses met his nose, as did the brush of her hair against his cheek. "They gave our reservation away. How do you feel about hitting the food trucks at South Port?"

The tenseness in her body testified that she didn't feel great about it, but Brad didn't know what else to do. At this time of night, every restaurant on the island would be busy.

"Or you have a restaurant on-site at the hotel, don't you?" he asked.

"We can't go there," she said, turning to exit the building. The burst of sunshine shocked Brad, almost like he'd forgotten it was still light outside inside the dim restaurant.

"Why not?"

"And it's an inn, not a hotel," she said over her shoulder.

Brad had seen her walk quickly in her heels, so it was no surprise that her stride in sandals was impressive. She ate up the distance back to the car, getting in before he could open her door.

"So no to the inn," he said, almost rolling his eyes.

"No," she said. "My family will see us."

"Isn't that what you wanted?" he asked, confused. "Oh, and I got you a ring."

"I don't necessarily want everyone to know we're engaged," she said. "But I think if you want to convince Carmen that we are, we'd better play the part for a little bit."

"Play the part," Brad said, putting the car in gear and backing out of the spot. The sky held a shade of gold that took his breath away, and he added, "Look at that sunset. It's gorgeous."

"I love watching the sun set," she said, her voice wistful.

"Me too." He glanced at her, thinking something as simple as a sunset would be the first thing they had in common. "The sunsets over the Gulf of Mexico were amazing."

"I'll bet." She gave him a smile, and he turned onto the road. Getting to South Port took some fancy driving and a huge tip to a valet who insisted their lot was already full. But finally, they each had a tray with a footlong corndog and seasoned potato logs, little packets of ketchup, and a spot on a long stone wall looking out at the water.

"Ah," Brad said as he sat down. "This is what dinner should be."

Celeste made a noise of disbelief, and she shook her head. Saying nothing, she ripped open one of her packets of ketchup, a squeal coming from her mouth in the next moment.

"What?" he asked, turning to look at her. Ketchup had splattered her face and the collar of her blouse.

He couldn't help the chuckles that came out of his mouth. "I'm sorry," he said, grabbing for an extra napkin. He started pawing at her blouse, only stopping when a growl came from her throat.

Brad dropped the napkin and pulled his hand back. "Sorry."

"You certainly sound like it," she said acidly, and Brad started laughing fully now.

"Really," he said. "Those ketchup packets can be lethal." He bypassed the condiments and ate his corndog with only the mustard he'd squeezed all over it.

Down the beach a ways, a band played, and several groups of people played games in the sand in front of them. A volleyball court sat to his left, and he watched the people batting the ball back and forth.

Brad usually didn't have trouble conversing with women, but he couldn't think of a single thing to say to Celeste. They ate in silence, and she wasn't bringing anything up either.

He'd just finished eating when a cry went up. "Heads!" someone yelled, and he automatically looked up to find the ball.

The white volleyball gleamed in the late evening light, and he said, "Watch out, Celeste," only a moment before sand sprayed everywhere.

Celeste screamed, and the volleyball bounced just behind her. The man that had been trying to get to it said, "I'm so sorry," and bent to pick up Brad's soda, which was covered in sand.

He handed it to him, and Brad looked at Celeste. She sat very still, both arms held out to her sides, her tray of food on her lap, completely inedible now.

She spit sand out of her mouth and started brushing herself off while horror moved through Brad. He wanted to help, but he didn't dare touch her again.

Celeste stood up and continued to pat herself down, trying to get the sand out of her hair and off her clothes. "Okay," she said after a moment. "I'm done. Take me home, please."

4

C eleste was grateful Brad didn't argue, and he didn't try to help de-sand her. He drove her home and walked her up to the front door. "Sorry everything sort of fell apart," he said.

She'd never had a worse date than this one, fake or not, and all she could do was look at him.

He dug in his pocket. "Did you want the ring?" He held it out to her, and she dropped her eyes to it. The gold band was thick, and it housed a diamond easily as big as her knuckle. The cut and setting might not be what she would've picked for herself, but as far as wedding rings went, it was great.

She took it and slid it on her own finger, and though their engagement wasn't real, Celeste couldn't help thinking this was the worst proposal in the history of weddings. And she planned them for a living.

Humiliation drove through her again, just like it had been for the past thirty minutes. She couldn't remember the last time she'd eaten a corndog on the beach—or been denied at Radish.

"We don't need to do this," he said.

Celeste looked at him. "Six weeks."

"Is that a counter-offer?"

"Maybe I'd like to have a fiancé this summer," she said, thinking of all the fun she could have on the island if she had a handsome man on her arm. She didn't have to marry him in the end. She was just tired of being alone, of waking Gwen when it was time for them to go to bed, of hoping one of her exes would text that day. So, so tired.

"Do you object?" She had several, but she kept them all dormant, because Brad looked like he was seriously considering the engagement.

His blue eyes flashed with fire. "Why me?"

"*You're* the one who asked me."

"I can just tell Carmen the truth."

"That woman will fillet you alive." Celeste started working the ring off her finger again. "But okay. You take it —" Her voice muted as his fingers came over hers, the warmth seeping into her skin.

"Keep it," he said. "And maybe we can try for a do-over at Radish tomorrow night."

Celeste didn't know what to say, but she stalled in taking off the ring. She had no idea where the words came from, but it was her voice that said, "Sure, let's try a do-over tomorrow night."

"Seven," he said. "I'll pick you up again." And with that, he gave her a salute and walked away. Celeste watched him go for the second time that day, wondering what she'd gotten herself into. Why she'd wanted to keep this ruse going with a man that was her total opposite.

CELESTE SLEPT LITTLE THAT NIGHT, AND DAWN FOUND HER in Gwen's chair on the screened-in back porch. Celeste had never excelled with extra time on her hands. She got too deep inside her mind if she didn't stay busy, and her string of texts proved it.

If we do this, I think we need some rules.

I have a couple in mind, and I'm open to suggestions.

What do you think?

She'd waited for a few minutes after sending those, actually surprised to get a response before she could continue. After all, it was barely six o'clock in the morning, and she hadn't pegged Brad for an early riser.

"Which is stupid," she told herself, glancing up and searching for the horizon line that marked the spot where the ocean met the land. She and Gwen didn't enjoy nearly the same beachfront property as Sheryl or Alissa, a couple of their sisters. "You barely know him at all."

Scratch that. She *didn't* know him at all. She knew he'd

grown up on the island, but he was a decade older than her, and six-year-olds weren't aware of jocks in high school. She knew he'd played professional football for a long time.

The control freak inside her wanted to do a search on the Internet, because it surely knew more about Bradley Keith than anyone or anything else. But the romantic in her wanted to get to know him the old-fashioned way.

Sure, rules, go, he'd sent.

Celeste's perfectly crafted rules from her sleepless night suddenly vanished. The old-fashioned way of dating and getting to know someone didn't require rules. Did it?

She straightened her shoulders and shook her head a little to make her hair swish. She'd dealt with difficult and stressful situations way harder than a fake engagement to a gorgeous former athlete.

"And now a small business owner," she reminded herself. Well, and Midnight, her black miniature poodle who was currently conked out beside her on the loveseat.

Six weeks, she typed. *Then we can end things. That gets us through the bulk of summer.* She sent the message, and before she could even start typing the next rule, he'd messaged back.

Does it?

Summer ends at the end of August here?

I mean, I've been gone for a while, but seems like it goes all the way to Halloween to me.

Celeste scoffed. "Halloween?"

No, she typed out. The Fall Festival on the island is always the third week of September.

Whatever you say, he said, and Celeste imagined him delivering it with a heavy dose of disbelief. Sarcasm. Mocking.

Rule 2: No touching unless we're in public. She sent the message, ignoring his rudeness. *She* was helping *him,* but in the back of her mind, she knew her perpetuation of this relationship had a lot to do with her too.

Fine, he sent.

Rule 3: No kissing.

At all?

At all.

That seems impossible, he said.

"Why would it be impossible?" Celeste asked as her fingers flew across the screen, typing out the same message.

What if I need to kiss you in public?

Why would anyone need to do that? Celeste had a personal vendetta against public displays of affection, and she could not imagine a situation where she'd kiss a man —and that included *any* man—in front of anyone else.

Let's recap a few facts, he said. *You grew up on this island and your whole family lives here. I grew up here and have plenty of friends and family too. Do you really think we're not going to have to work a little bit to convince them that we really are engaged?*

Celeste read his message, and then reread it. She

relaxed so that her phone rested on her lap, and one hand reached over to absently stroke Midnight. She needed the dog's comfort, and she made a small groan and stretched out her back legs as Celeste patted her.

"He's right," she said, but she didn't want to admit it. She'd have a few days before her sisters knew about her new boyfriend, and she'd have to have an explanation for the diamond on her finger.

She glanced down at it, as she hadn't taken it off yet.

Fine, she typed out. *Rule 3 is scratched.*

Any others? he asked, and Celeste appreciated that he didn't gloat or make a big deal out of being right.

If I think of more, I'll let you know.

Do you have any? she asked.

Wear the ring all the time, he said. *And tell as few lies as possible.*

A pang of regret hit Celeste's heart. She didn't go around lying to people either. Besides Gwen, she didn't see her sisters all that much. And sometimes she and Gwen felt like ships passing in the night. In fact, her sister had already gone to the inn, which was why Celeste could have this texting conversation in private.

All right, she sent to Brad. She wanted to invite him to eat lunch with her, but they already had a dinner date, and she didn't want to seem desperate.

She wasn't desperate.

She was helping *him.*

He was not her real fiancé.

Maybe if she repeated those facts to herself enough, she'd be able to stick her rules.

"I have one more rule, just for myself," she whispered to Midnight. "Don't fall in love with him for real."

Celeste had always been very good at following the rules. So could only hope that winning streak could continue, because while Brad rubbed her the wrong way right now, she suspected he might be able to change that pretty quickly. After all, he was handsome, and rich, and a Carter's Cove boy. Everything Celeste had always wanted.

5

B rad got out of the shower, expecting a dozen more texts from Celeste outlining a few more rules she'd like to see for their relationship.

The letters had jumbled, but he'd been able to put them together after a few minutes. Didn't mean her rules made sense.

He conjured up the beautiful blonde in his mind as he shaved. He could admit she was beautiful. But wow, she needed a beach vacation to take down her professionalism. He wondered what she'd look like without all the makeup, the perfectly positioned jewelry, the tight pencil skirts.

She had worn jeans last night, and Brad secretly found himself hoping she'd wear those again. Or maybe he liked the skirts.

"You don't like any of it," he told his reflection. He'd

once been wound as tight as Celeste, and his doctor had put him on blood pressure medication to get him out of the danger zone for a heart attack.

He'd calmed down after that. Let his manager take care of some things while he focused on just breathing. That was what Celeste needed to do, and being with her might just put him over the edge.

He dressed and left the house, wishing he had a dog to say good-bye to. Even a cat, though Brad had never understood the value of felines before. He had a moment of missing the dogs and horses on the farm in Lexington, and he had the thought to call his grandfather. See how the operation was doing. He'd *loved* going to Kentucky in the spring and summer to work the thoroughbred farm with his granddad, and he often wondered if he should've gone there after retiring from football.

You still can, he told himself. Projects would conclude, and he didn't need to sign on more jobs. The thought mulling around inside his mind, he got behind the wheel of his truck, thinking he needed to get a motorcycle to be able to manage the summertime crowds. Of course, he'd thought that last year too, and he still had the king-cab-sized truck he practically needed a ladder to get into. He could've taken the convertible, but it wasn't conducive to construction sites.

He'd never learned to cook, so he breakfasted each morning at Sunny's, the chime on the door twinkling his arrival.

"Morning, Brad," Cindi said, not even bothering to pluck a menu from the pile before she led him to a small table in front of the window. "Coffee or hot chocolate today?"

"Hot chocolate," he said, already feeling wound up from the early-morning text-fest with Celeste. She'd woken him, as he didn't usually go to his construction sites until a more normal hour, but he kept his phone on twenty-four-seven in case of emergencies. Things flooded and sparked, and he'd learned the hard way to be reachable.

"Comin' up." Cindi walked away, and Brad pulled out his phone. He ate alone every morning, unless he'd specifically asked one of his foremen to join him so they could talk about a project. He read the Internet headlines, checked his email, and kept up with the Falcons. That would take him through when his food came, and then he put his screens away while he ate.

Darius had emailed, and Brad smiled at his phone as he read his friend's recap of a family vacation. Darius still played professional football, and their off-season wasn't very long. He'd taken his wife and kids to Italy for a few weeks, and apparently, they'd gone to a beach where clothing was optional.

Brad chuckled to himself, tapped out a quick response, and glanced up when his hot chocolate came. "Morning, honey," Karen said with a smile. "How's your mama?"

"Just fine, ma'am," he said, his southern roots slipping into his mouth. "It's her birthday next week." Even as he said it, horror hit him. His mother's birthday. It would be normal to take a fiancée to that, wouldn't it?

A sigh filled his whole soul, and Karen cocked her head as part of it came out of his mouth. "You okay, honey? What're you having today?"

"The Big Ben," he said. "Extra bacon."

"Double eggs?"

"Yes." As if he'd ever passed on the double eggs.

"All right." She walked away, and Brad returned his attention to his phone. He should call his mother, but he ended up dialing Bella, his younger sister.

"Hey," she said just as a wail filled the line. "Just a sec." Scuffling and crying came through the line. Bella spoke to her daughter in a harsh tone, and told her to find her shoes and put them on.

Things quieted, and she said, "Sorry about that. Annie lost her elephant, and that means the world has ended." Bella sighed, and it sounded like it held the weight of the world. Her husband had been deployed for six months, and Bella was doing the single mom thing the best way she could.

"I can take the kids this afternoon," he said. "Would they want to go to the water park for a couple of hours?"

"You would be my hero if you did that."

"Consider it done," he said. "Maybe like two or so? I... have a date at seven." He pushed the last words out in a

huge rush, hoping Bella would be so tired and over-
whelmed that she'd just keep talking about the water park
on the island.

"I'll make sure they're ready," she said, and Brad felt
like he'd dodged a speeding lineman. "Then I can get
some work done on the computer in peace."

"You still working for that airline?"

"Every day," she said. "Who are you going out with?"

"Uh, Celeste Heartwood?"

"Celeste Heartwood?" The incredulity in Bella's voice
wasn't hard to hear. "Wow, Brad."

"You don't have to say it like that."

"Like what?"

"Like she's way out of my league. I already know
she is."

"You have such a warped sense of who you are."

"I know who I am," Brad said. And he was simple. He
didn't care what anyone thought of him. He liked working
out and working with his hands. So football and construction came naturally to him. He liked the tranquility of the
beach in the morning before all the tourists showed up,
and he liked the rolling hills of Kentucky.

"Listen, I called about Mom's party next week," he
said. "Do you think I could bring Celeste?"

"Depends," Bella said. "On how serious it is."

Brad thought of the diamond ring he'd given the
woman last night. "It's pretty serious."

"And this is the first we're hearing about it?"

"I mean, I'm not famous here."

"Are you kidding me right now?" She spoke to her son, and Brad was glad her attention was divided. "Everyone knows who you are, Brad. I have at least three women every week ask me if you're dating anyone."

"Well, tell them I am," he said, his mouth suddenly so dry. "What do you think of the party?"

"It's up to you. Mom and Dad are weird about significant others."

Yes, they were. In fact, his older brother David had gotten engaged just so he could bring his girlfriend on a family cruise one year.

"Great, I'll see you later." Brad ended the call before he could get asked another question about the seriousness of his relationship with Celeste.

My mom's birthday party is next week, he started typing in a text to Celeste, having to delete some of the words a couple of times to fix them. He could spell, but sometimes letters didn't line up right for him. *Thursday night. Are you available?*

He half-hoped she wouldn't be. Then he wouldn't have to involve his family in the charade.

I'll check my schedule when I get to work, she messaged back, his phone chiming loudly in the restaurant. He moved to silence it as Karen showed up with his food.

"Big Ben," she said, setting down a plate laden with hash browns, eggs, and French toast. A plate of pancakes followed, along with, "Extra bacon. And I'll get you another hot chocolate."

"Thanks, Karen," he said, flipping his phone over and setting it aside.

"I'm sure it'll be fine," a woman said over someone else, and Brad looked up to see what the ruckus was about.

Celeste stood there, and Brad scrambled to his feet. "See?" she said to Cindi. "He's expecting me."

Brad wasn't, but he threw Cindi a look that said it was okay, and he awkwardly stepped into Celeste's personal space. "Hey, beautiful," he said, almost choking on the words, even if they were true. "I must not have gotten the message you were coming. I didn't tell Cindi." He pressed his lips to her cheek, surprised at how...good it felt. A spark ran down his neck, and he pulled back quickly. His eyes met Celeste's, and she seemed as surprised as him.

"I've already ordered," he said helplessly, dragging his gaze from hers to his spread of food that filled the whole table.

Karen appeared, and it was a tight fit with all of them standing. Brad wondered if he'd ever have a normal encounter with Celeste, and he gestured to the other side of the table. "Sit, sit."

"Anything for you, honey?" Karen asked.

"Just coffee, please," she said. "With sugar and cream. And real cream. Not these little cups." She looked up at Karen. "Do you have real cream?"

Brad wanted to crawl under the table, and this woman had accomplished something he hadn't thought possible: she'd made his appetite disappear.

"Coffee," Karen repeated in a deadpan. "Be right back."

Celeste unlooped her purse from over her shoulder and settled into her seat before looking at Brad. "I heard your phone go off when I texted you back."

"What are you doing here?" he asked. This didn't seem like the type of place a woman like her would frequent. The inn surely had room service, and they had a little bakery in the back too. He knew it was good—he'd eaten his second breakfast there a couple of times.

"Sunny's has the best croissants," Celeste said matter-of-factly. "I ordered a bunch for a client we have coming in today." She smiled at him, and Brad couldn't help smiling back.

He ducked his head a moment later, because he wasn't supposed to like this woman. He picked up his fork and started pushing his eggs around his plate. They needed ketchup, so he reached for the bottle.

"You like ketchup on eggs?" she asked.

"Yes, ma'am," he said, lifting his eyes to hers.

Time seemed to slow. "Me too." Celeste smiled again, dropped her own chin, and tucked her hair behind her ear. "Maybe we will have some things in common."

6

Celeste couldn't believe the balloon of hope expanding inside her chest. She and Brad seemed so different on the outside. Sure, he was refined in a different kind of way. He'd obviously gotten up and showered and ready for the day. He was employed. He had money. But he surely used those little cups of fake creamer, and Celeste didn't.

But they both liked sunsets, and now they both liked ketchup on their eggs.

"So it's your mom's birthday," she said, trying to get a conversation going. The man had food enough for three people in front of him, and it was obvious she'd interrupted a morning ritual he had.

"Yes," he said. "Next week. My brother is coming in from Kentucky and everything."

"Wow," she said.

"Yeah." Brad nodded and reached for his mug.

He wasn't drinking coffee, and that surprised Celeste. "What does your brother do in Kentucky?"

"My grandfather owns a two-hundred-and-twenty acre thoroughbred farm," he said over the top of his mug. "David runs that with my uncle."

"Fascinating," Celeste said.

"Do you like horses?" Brad asked.

"I mean, I don't know."

"You know you can ride ponies in the ocean, right?" he asked. "It's awesome."

"I've heard of it," she said coolly.

"We should do it," he said. "I love horses, and it's been a while since I've been on the sea ponies."

Celeste took an extra moment to take a deep breath. "I've never done it."

"You've lived on Carter's Cove your whole life and have never ridden the sea ponies?" He didn't have to sound so surprised. Maybe even exasperated.

"Nope," Celeste said, choosing to keep the moment light. "So we should do it."

"You check your calendar," he said, looking at his pancakes as he smeared them with all that delicious butter. Celeste decided she'd order breakfast from the kitchen when she got to the inn. "And let me know."

"Deal," she said, sliding out of the booth. "Okay, Bradley. I'll see you tonight, okay?"

He grinned at her and nodded, and Celeste was

supremely glad he couldn't see beneath skin and bone to the way her pulse bobbed in her chest. That smile... yeah, that smile was downright dangerous to her health.

"I'M JUST SAYING, YOU NEVER EAT BREAKFAST," GWEN SAID. "And you were wearing perfume last night when you got me up to go to bed."

Celeste cut another triangle of pancake and put it in her mouth, buying herself some time before she had to speak. Of all of her sisters, she was closest to Gwen. Their relationship was why they could live together and not kill one another.

"I had a date," she finally said, hitting the T in "date" hard.

Gwen just blinked at her, her eyes widening slightly. "Tell me it wasn't with Andre."

"Nope."

"Boyd? Because you *promised* you wouldn't go out with him again."

"It wasn't Boyd."

Gwen gasped and covered her mouth. "Ben?" came through her fingers.

"No," Celeste said emphatically. "No, none of them. No one I've ever been out with before." And Celeste couldn't help feeling proud of that, even though a small pinch in the back of her heart reminded her that it hadn't been a real date.

"Who is it, then?" Gwen asked, reaching for Celeste's fork. Her sister didn't eat breakfast either, so to have a plate of pancakes between them felt magical, like Christmas morning. Her mother had always made pancakes and eggs on Christmas morning.

"Okay, don't die," Celeste said. "And you can't tell anyone. Not even Teagan."

"Why would I tell Teagan? It's not like he knows everything about me." Gwen's face turned red, though, and Celeste knew her head chef in the kitchen absolutely got to know everything about Gwen and her life.

"I don't want anyone else to know," Celeste said. She didn't see Olympia, Alissa, or Sheryl that much. If she could contain Brad to just Gwen, the chances of her being able to get out of the engagement without involving a lot of her family members would be higher.

"Fine, fine," Gwen said. "I only see Alissa and Olympia, and...maybe you shouldn't tell me." She looked like she might cry. "I'm not great with secrets."

She really wasn't, but Celeste really wanted to tell someone. "Alissa will be opening her shop soon, right?" Celeste asked. Her younger sister had rented a shop on Main Street and would be opening her own fish monger shop very soon. The inn had just hired Sheryl's boyfriend at their head baker, which actually annoyed Celeste.

Gage was the best security guard on the island, and

she'd used him for multiple weddings and events at The Heartwood Inn. After all, the wedding crashers who tried to get a two-hundred-dollar meal for free required someone with big muscles and a no-nonsense attitude, both of which Gage possessed.

How he and Sheryl had made things work was a mystery to Celeste. At the same time, she seized onto the differences between the bodyguard and her sister, using them to make an even stronger case for her and Brad.

"Yes, next week, I think," Gwen said. "I think Friday."

"I'm busy Thursday," Celeste said. "So I hope it's not then."

Gwen didn't ask what Celeste had on Thursday, though that would've been the perfect segue into talking about her new boyfriend. Fiancé. Date. Whatever Brad was. He certainly wasn't to boyfriend status yet, as Celeste had a rule for that. A man didn't get that label until she kissed him, and while Brad had said her no-kissing rule was impossible, Celeste still wasn't sure.

He had kissed her on the cheek at Sunny's, and Celeste took the fork back from her sister so she could distract herself with pancakes.

"Maybe just give me a hint of who you're seeing," Gwen said as she stood up. "I have to get back to work, and it'll give me something to think about."

"Besides Teagan, you mean."

Gwen rolled her eyes. "The man barely knows I exist."

"You sign his paychecks. He knows you exist."

"But not outside of the kitchen, he doesn't," Gwen said, her voice taking on a wistful quality. "It's fine. I don't have a crush on him anymore. He's actually kind of annoying."

"I'm sure he is," Celeste said. "And the hint is he grew up here on the island, left for a while, and is back."

Gwen grinned, her mind already working if the glint in her eye said anything, and waved as she left Celeste's office.

She couldn't help sighing as she put one more bite of pancake in her mouth. Then she needed to get to work. Focus on something besides the dashingly handsome former football player...who she was engaged to.

After pushing the remainder of her pancakes away, she opened her top desk drawer where she'd stored the ring. She didn't need to wear it at work—unless she wanted to alert her sisters and her assistant to her recent relationship status change.

And she didn't.

Not yet.

One of Brad's rules was to wear the ring, but she didn't need to do that until they went out. Another of his was to lie to as few people as possible, and storing the ring in the top desk drawer did that.

"Paige," she said into the intercom. "Can you bring me the Brandsen files? I have them on my to-do list this morning."

"Sure thing." A few moments later, Paige appeared in

the doorway. She put the files on Celeste's desk with, "What's all this?"

"Pancakes," Celeste said. "You can have them. I'm done."

"I thought we were having lunch together." The brunette folded her arms and lifted her eyebrows at Celeste. "You have something to tell me about that guy that stopped by yesterday."

"Do I?" Celeste flipped open one of the folders Paige had brought.

"Yes." Paige sat down in the chair across from Celeste. "I already ordered cheesesteaks from House. You can't back out now." She sang the last few words, and Celeste giggled.

She abandoned the paperwork, though she really did have so much to do, and said, "Okay, fine. But I really have to get something done first."

"Oh, yeah, of course," Paige said, standing up. Her heels clicked on the industrial carpet as she walked toward the door. "I'll leave you alone to do that."

"Great," Celeste said to herself. Now it was time to get to work.

"Henry Sylvester," Gwen guessed from the kitchen. Celeste had come home early from work again, and this time, Gwen wasn't already asleep on the back porch.

"Ew, no." Celeste bent to set the food bowl down for
Midnight. "There you go, sweets. Eat your dinner." With
Gwen awake, she'd see Brad when he showed up in only
thirty minutes.

"He's the only one left," Gwen said, a definite whine in
her voice. "You've said no to every man I've said for the
past half-hour."

"There's one more," Celeste assured her.

"Just tell me then." Gwen slid her grilled cheese sandwich onto a plate, her eyes wide and filled with curiosity.

Celeste really wanted to tell her. "You can't tell
anyone."

"We've already established that I won't. I don't have
anyone to tell."

"That's not true, Gwenny. You have your bunko group.
And your sea kayaking group."

"And we don't talk about men," Gwen fired back. "It's
actually a rule in the bunko group."

And Celeste liked rules. "Okay," she said. "You're going
to meet him in a minute anyway." She'd opted for an
elegant-yet-flirty sundress for their second attempt at
Radish, and she adjusted one of the wide straps on her
shoulder, the weight of the engagement ring in the pocket
almost too heavy to carry.

"It's Bradley Keith." She couldn't keep the smile off her
face as she said it.

"You're kidding!" Gwen shrieked and ran over to hug

Celeste as if she knew about the engagement and thought it was real.

Celeste wanted to tell her, but her sister didn't really have a lot of opportunities to interact with people, and she wanted the secret for one more night.

Now, if only tonight would be more successful than last night. And honestly? That wouldn't be hard to do, and her trepidation returned.

7

Brad's stomach squirmed like he'd swallowed live snakes as he walked up Celeste's front sidewalk. Somewhere in her garden, crickets sang, and he wished he was as content. The woman had been on his mind for hours, and he hadn't even cared that another delay at his construction site across the channel that separated Carter's Cove from the mainland would set him back a week.

Didn't even *care*.

He wasn't sure how the woman had wormed her way under his skin so quickly. Sure, she was beautiful, but he knew outward beauty could only go so far. He'd noticed that she hadn't been wearing the engagement band at breakfast that morning, and he'd been stewing over her rules ever since.

He knocked, and another blonde opened the door

barely two seconds later. Her sister—and she'd clearly been anticipating him. His heart twisted, but he put his professional football smile on his face. "Hello," he said. "I'm here for Celeste."

"Celeste," she said at the same time as him, her smile so wide it had to hurt. "Come in. I'm Gwen, her sister. She's just doing something with Midnight."

Brad stepped into the house, because it was air conditioned and the front porch was not. Plus, Celeste had not invited him in last night, either before or after the date. "Midnight?" he asked.

"Her dog." Gwen closed the door behind him. "She's a little miniature poodle. Cutest thing ever." The back door opened, drawing their attention, and Gwen added, "There they are. Celeste, your date is here." She strode through the living room to the kitchen.

Brad looked around the house quickly. It was perfectly spotless—he'd expect no less from Celeste—and smelled like lilacs and lavender. Or some other kind of womanly flower. His eyes landed on Celeste, and he couldn't look away.

He felt transfixed by her soft curls as they draped over her nearly bare shoulders. Tonight, she wore a long, flowing dress that still somehow broadcasted all her female features. Brad could barely breathe, but at least her gaze seemed locked in his too.

"Hey," she said, coming toward him. He slicked his palms down the front of his jeans so he wouldn't touch her with sweaty hands. She stooped and scooped up a little black dog. "This is my pup, Midnight." She stopped a few feet from him, and Brad leaned forward to pat the dog.

"She's so cute," he said. "I miss having a dog."

"You like dogs?" Her blue eyes sparkled like the ocean under sunlight, and Brad wanted to dive right in.

"Sure," he said. "My grandpa had a ton of dogs on the horse farm. There was this one named Reggie that chose me to be his human." Brad smiled just thinking about the little corgi. "He'd sleep with me, follow me all over the farm while I worked, chase the footballs I threw." He mentally commanded himself to stop talking.

"I thought you were a running back," she said, setting the dog down.

"I was a tight end," he said.

"I don't know what that means." Celeste put her arm in his and said, "See you later, Gwen."

"Bye," her sister said from her position in the kitchen, her eyes missing nothing. Brad wondered how many texts the woman could send in a minute, and he was willing to be it was a lot.

He turned and opened the door, leading Celeste through it. "You told her about us?"

"Yes," she said simply. "But only that we were going out. Nothing about the engagement." She said the words so smoothly, and Brad envied her for that.

"Okay," he said, moving down the steps. "And a tight

end is larger and slower than a running back. I was a receiver—I caught the ball. Or I was used as a lineman for the running backs."

"Larger and slower." She paused so he could open the car door for her. He'd brought the convertible again, but tonight, the top was up. "You can put the top down."

"Can I? Last night, you seemed like it bothered you."

She reached into her dress pocket and pulled out a hair band. "I'll just put my hair up." She gathered it into a quick ponytail and secured it. She beamed at him like she'd achieved something great, and maybe she had.

Brad had never seen the woman wear her hair up, so maybe this was a big step for her. He opened the door for her and watched her sit in his car. As he walked around the back of it, he closed his eyes and prayed with everything he had that tonight would go well.

For some reason, he really wanted Celeste to like him. Sure, maybe they only had six weeks, and then they'd go their separate ways. But he didn't want to be miserable for the next six weeks.

He started the car and pushed the button to put the top down. Celeste had put on a pair of oversized sunglasses that made her look like a sexy celebrity or some sort of exotic royal. He backed out of the driveway and headed for the part of the island where Radish waited for them.

He'd called three times that day to make sure his

reservation would be ready. Bradley Keith. Two people. Seven-thirty.

"You don't seem larger or slower than the other men I've dated," she said, and Brad swung his attention to her.

"I—" He had no idea what to say. He found something funny about what she'd said, and he started laughing.

Celeste giggled too. "That sounded weird, didn't it?"

"A little," he said, still chuckling. "How many guys have you gone out with that play professional football?"

"You would be the first."

"You must be dating giants then," he said. "If I'm not bigger than them." He was, and he knew it. She did too. He couldn't buy a suit off the rack, and he had to special order his shoes. He was tall, and broad, and if she hadn't dated a professional athlete before, he was definitely bigger than her other boyfriends.

"Not dating giants," she said, putting her hand over the top of the door and letting the wind push against it. "Just losers."

"Ah," he said. "Well, we almost won the Super Bowl a couple of years ago. But I never did, so I guess, technically, I'm a loser too."

"You know what I mean," she said.

"Do I?" he asked, slowing for a stop sign. He checked traffic and then looked directly at her. "Maybe you better tell me what makes a loser for Celeste Heartwood. I'm sure you have a list."

She opened her mouth, and Brad saw the moment his words hit her—and hurt her.

"I'm sorry," he said quickly. "That was rude. I'm sorry."

"Rudeness," she said, turning away from him. "Definitely makes the list."

"I'm sorry," he said for a third time. "It's just...you weren't wearing the ring at breakfast, and you're not wearing it now, and I thought maybe the rules had already been thrown out the window."

She reached into her purse and produced the ring, sliding it neatly onto her fourth finger.

"Okay," he said. "So what else makes the list for being a loser?"

"Unemployment," she said, her voice carrying a bit of sarcasm.

"Oh, I have a job, sweetheart."

"Not able to commit," she said as if he hadn't spoken.

He'd been engaged twice. He could commit. Brad said nothing as the sign for Radish appeared up ahead, the letters swimming before settling into their proper places.

"Unable to compromise," she said. "Flirting with other women while we're out. Having more than one girlfriend. Expecting me to pay for everything. Asking for free rooms at the inn."

Brad looked at her. "Wow, Celeste. Have men really done those things to you?" He wanted to smack them all upside the head. Shout at them that they had someone amazing right in front of them, and how dare they treat her like that?

The thoughts made his throat tighten, because did he really think she was amazing?

Yes, he thought. She was. Maybe she wasn't exactly his type, but that didn't make her less than wonderful.

"Yes," she said. "Every guy I've ever dated."

"Well, maybe you've been dating the wrong type of men." He pulled into the Radish drive-through to let the valet take the car. Their conversation stalled as he got out and walked over to her side of the car to let her out.

He appreciated that she gave him the chance to be a gentleman, and as she laced her arm through his again, an electric thrill ran up his arm and across his shoulders.

"I've only dated men from Carter's Cove," she said. "So if I stop doing that, there's only tourists left."

"Or men who grew up here, left, and came back," he said without missing a beat. He smiled at the man who opened the door for them and moved right past all the people waiting to the hostess station. "Bradley Keith," he said. "I have a reservation."

The same woman from last night looked up from her complicated chart and said, "Of course. Right this way, Mister Keith."

Oh, so tonight it was *Mister Keith*. Whatever. He secured his hand in Celeste's and followed the hostess to a quiet, private booth out of the way of foot traffic. "This is great," he said. "Thank you."

Once he'd sat down, she handed him his menu and then Celeste's before walking away. He flipped it open as if he'd really read it. He could read. Of course he could. He'd made it through college with tutors and extra help. Everything just took so long, though, and he hated that even going to dinner was a chore for him.

Their waiter arrived with a bottle of wine and another man who poured water for them into two glasses. "Wine tonight?" the waiter asked, and Brad looked at Celeste. He wouldn't have any, as he was driving. That, and he'd never acquired a taste for alcohol, despite his grandfather's best efforts to educate him about bourbon. Or maybe *because* of that harrowing experience where the whiskey had burned his nose and throat for hours.

"None for me, thanks," she said. "But I would love one of your frozen raspberry lemon virgins." She smiled at him with all the power of a princess, and Brad realized she'd completely mesmerized him.

He cleared his throat as he looked away. "I'll have a Coke," he said. Totally normal. Mundane. Laid back. That was just how he was.

"I'll get those drinks in," he said. "Would you like to hear the specials?"

"Definitely," Brad said, because that was what he'd order. No menu needed. If there was a steak option—and at a place as fancy as Radish, there would be—he'd get that.

The waiter started rattling off their fresh fish of the

day, "locally caught by Carter's Cove's own Alissa Heart-wood," and a sausage risotto that actually sounded good. He finished, and said, "I'll be back with the drinks and to take your orders."

"Is that your sister?" Brad asked, though he already knew it was.

"Alissa, yes," Celeste said, unwrapping her silverware and placing her napkin on her lap. "She's actually opening her own fish monger shop next week."

"That's great," he said, truly meaning it. "What does she do right now?"

"She's the head baker at the inn. We all work there."

"But she won't, after she opens the shop." Brad watched her, looking for signs of what that meant for the family.

"Right," Celeste said, utterly nonplussed. "But my other sister's boyfriend is taking over the job."

"I see. Do significant others have to work for the inn?"

"Of course not."

"Because I heard a rumor that Olympia's boyfriend is a consultant for Heartwood."

Celeste narrowed her eyes. "Where did you hear that?"

Brad wanted to pull at his collar, but he reached for his water glass instead. "Nowhere."

Leaning back in her seat, she folded her arms and glared at him. Brad chuckled, because it was actually kind of fun to see her irritation.

"I'm doing a penthouse remodel at the Kipton Monoco," he said. "I overheard the manager talking about Chet. He wasn't happy that he was at Heartwood." He gave her a small shrug. "That's all."

"Well, he shouldn't be happy," Celeste said. "Chet's smart, and we're glad to have him."

"I'm sure you are."

"And it's not true about having to work for us," she said, still plenty of bite in her tone. "Alissa's boyfriend doesn't do anything for the inn."

"Noted," he said, wishing he could drown himself in the water glass. "So, Celeste." He exhaled heavily. "What do you do for fun?"

"Fun?" she repeated, as if she didn't understand the meaning of the word.

"Right," he said. "Fun. For example, I like to fly kites on the beach. When it's really windy, it's awesome." He smiled at her, almost the way he would a scared child who was nervous to meet him. And he'd experienced that before, as the Florida Falcons did a ton of community outreach programs, especially in the lower income neighborhoods in Tampa.

"I like to watch documentaries," she said, reaching up tucking her hair behind her ear. She became soft in that moment, and Brad watched all of the anger and annoyance flow out of her.

"You'd get along with my brother-in-law," he said. "Bella's husband? She's closer to Olympia's age, but her husband loves documentaries. Especially historical stuff."

Celeste nodded, those blue eyes back to sparkling instead of searing. Their drinks arrived, and he ordered the steak special while she pointed to the menu and ordered a chicken dish he'd never heard of.

With that done, she lifted her bright pink concoction to her lips, and Brad's body burst into flames watching her sip it. "Mm," she said, her eyes drifting closed. "I love this drink."

His phone buzzed in his pocket, and he took it out. "I have to keep it on for work," he said. "I have five active construction sites right now. Do you mind if I check it?"

"Of course not," she said, swirling her straw in her drink.

But it wasn't a job-related text. Horror still struck him in the heart, and he sucked in a breath.

"What?" Celeste asked, but Brad couldn't speak. He just slid the phone across the table to her. She held his gaze for another breath, and then looked at the phone.

He closed his eyes, Bella's text ingrained on the backs of his eyelids.

You're ENGAGED?? Call me right now!

8

"Well, so much for that secret," Celeste said, her heart somewhere in the bottom of her stomach.

"How do you think she found out?" he asked. "You haven't told anyone, right?"

"No one," she confirmed. "You?"

"No one," he said. "I don't have a ton of friends anyway."

"I have my assistant," Celeste said. "And I did tell her about you today over lunch. But just because you stopped by yesterday, and I didn't mention that we were dating. I didn't wear the ring at the office." Her nerves skipped around her bloodstream, though she'd known this would happen. Nothing stayed a secret on Carter's Cove for long, even though more than half of the population consisted of tourists right now.

"What should I do?"

"Call her if you want." Celeste pushed his phone back toward him. She'd just wanted one more night of them being a secret. Who had told his sister? She'd been wearing the ring for maybe twenty minutes.

"I'm not calling her on our date," he said, tucking his phone back in his pocket. He looked at her again, and with the dim lighting, she couldn't really tell what he was thinking or feeling. She knew she was a tangled mess inside, going from miffed one moment to sighing the next.

If she had a list for the type of man she liked, Bradley Keith would check all the boxes. Of course, he'd marked one on her rude list too—and he'd quickly apologized.

Three times, she told herself. Andre had never apologized for anything, and he'd left her stranded at the ferry station on the mainland once. Not a single sorry had ever left that man's lips—and she'd gone out with him for months, broken up with him, and then gone out with him *again*.

So Brad apologizing three times in the span of sixty seconds was a vast improvement.

"There's a music festival this weekend," he said, and Celeste perked up. "Would you like to go with me?"

She blinked, sure this wasn't her reality. "I'd really like that," she said.

"Are you okay?" he asked. "I mean, we knew people were going to find out."

"I know." She sighed. "I feel like maybe I should've

told my family first, though, you know?" She nodded toward his jacket pocket. "Like, your sister seems mad."

"So maybe we just need to tell them."

Celeste felt torn right in half. Her parents still lived on the island, and she was close with them. Her father had just been over to fix the toilet for her and Gwen. "I thought we were going to lie as little as possible."

"So what do I tell Bella? No, it's not true?"

Celeste had seen plenty of movies with fake engagements. It would work out. "No, we need to go along with it. It's six weeks. Then we'll just break up, like we decided."

"I wish I'd never gone out with Carmen," he said miserably.

"Tell me about the engagement that only lasted six weeks," Celeste said, as she had dozens of questions for this man seated across from her.

"That would be the one to Tamara."

"There's more than one?" Celeste had no idea such a public figure could have so many private details. And even more surprising was she wanted to know every one of them. The good, the bad, the ugly.

He considered her for a moment. "Did you ever meet with a bride named Emily Taylor?"

Celeste cocked her head, the image of the cute blonde popping immediately into her mind's eye. "Yes," she said.

"She was my fiancée too," he said. "She called things off after a couple of months."

"Why?"

"Well, let's see," he said, exhaling. A chuckle followed. "I didn't know tonight was going to be a confessional."

"You don't have to say," Celeste said, reaching for her mocktail again. But oh, she wanted to know.

"Tamara and I had been together for a long time. It was the next step to get engaged and then married. So I asked her. A few weeks into it, she said I was married to my job, which I'll admit. I kind of was. That engagement lasted six weeks, and she hadn't even chosen a date yet. I don't think she liked me very much. She liked the *idea* of me. The idea of being a professional football player's wife. That kind of thing."

"That must've been hard."

"It wasn't easy," he agreed.

Celeste appreciated how vulnerable he was, which was another surprise for her. He clearly knew how to put his best foot forward, what with the sexy suit coat jacket over that white shirt but paired with jeans. The dazzling smile. The perfectly sculpted hair. Yes, he was dashing and charming in all the right ways, yet also laid back in a way Celeste envied.

"So that was the shorter one. Emily and I...we knew each other growing up. She has a couple of kids, and when I moved back here, we reconnected. We were friends more than anything, and I guess it made sense to ask her to marry me?"

"Did you just phrase that as a question?" Celeste asked.

"I did." He chuckled. "It was obvious we weren't going to get married. She called it off before things got too out of hand, thankfully."

"Yeah, thankfully," Celeste said. "So do you want to get married?"

He coughed over his soda and lifted his napkin to his mouth. "This is really forward talk for a first date," he teased.

She giggled and ducked her head. "I mean, in general."

"Yeah," he said. "Of course. You?"

Their eyes met, and Celeste felt something powerful move between them. "Yes," she said. "I want to get married. But I don't want it to be because we're friends or the man feels like he has to ask me because that's the next step in our relationship. I want him to be so passionately in love with me, he can't wait to make me his wife and spend his life with me."

Silence filled the space between them, and embarrassment heated Celeste's face. She looked away and cleared her throat. "Unfortunately, I've only been dating losers. So, needless to say, this is my first engagement."

Brad got up and came around the table, sending another dose of surprise through her. He put his arm around her in the small space, and pressed his lips to her forehead. "I'm sure you'll get a man exactly like that one day, Celeste."

She leaned into him, because he was strong and warm

and it felt so nice to have someone reassure her that she was worth a man like that.

A COUPLE OF DAYS PASSED, AND CELESTE DIDN'T PHYSICALLY see Brad. They sure did text a lot, and he made her laugh and smile while he wasn't even present. That was a definitely plus for the man, and she couldn't wait until the music festival.

She woke one morning, because her stupid phone wouldn't stop buzzing. Her heart zinged around in her chest. Maybe something had happened to her grand-mother. She'd fallen and broken a hip last year, and now she lived with Celeste's parents.

Her pulse skipping, she swiped on the conversation to see a long text string from her sisters. Alissa had started it, of course, as the woman went fishing at three-thirty in the morning.

Well, Celeste had been up almost that late texting her not-real-fiancé, and she didn't appreciate the early-morning texts—especially when she saw they'd been talking about her. Olympia had convinced the head chef at Redfin to cater for their private party using Alissa's fish, which was sweet.

But she wanted to know a head count, and she'd invited significant others. Celeste almost rolled her eyes. Why couldn't she just say boyfriends?

Assume 2 for Celeste, Alissa had said. I heard she was seeing Boyd again.

"Ew," Celeste said, though she had texted Boyd as late as last week.

I thought it was Ben, Olympia had sent.

"Double ew," Celeste said to herself. Ben was so boring. No, he didn't cheat on her, but he didn't do anything and that was almost worse.

At least it's not Andre, Sheryl had said, and then Gwen —the traitor had said the exact same thing.

It's definitely not Ben, Alissa said, and they'd finally stopped talking about her pathetic love life.

"Just wait until you show up with Bradley Keith," she said, practically stabbing at the screen as she typed them all a message.

It's not Ben, and it's six-freaking-AM! Celeste sent. I thought Grandma had fallen and broken another hip. Jeez.

Just mute notifications, Olympia said, as if Celeste didn't know how to use her phone. Her phone had been on vibrate, but she kept all of her jewelry out, and when the phone shook, so did the gold.

How many for you then? Gwen asked.

Put me down for two, Celeste said. Since I'm up already.

Who are you bringing? Alissa asked, and Celeste paused.

She had the perfect opportunity to tell them. Right now. Before word got out around the island about the engagement. But the party was in only a couple of days—

before the music festival. She had time. And what an entrance she'd make....

Her decision made, she answered, *I'll surprise you*, and swung her legs over the edge of the bed. Since she was up, she might as well do something. And the first thing she did was dive for her phone again and text Gwen to keep her mouth shut about Brad.

Of course I will, Gwen said. You said not to tell anyone, and I didn't. It was hard, though!

Celeste smiled and shook her head before she went to get in the shower.

An hour later, she knocked on her mother's door at the same time she went inside the beach house. "Ma," she said, feeling happier today than she had in a long time.

"Hello, darling," her mother said. "What's in that bag?" She lifted her coffee mug to her lips. If there was a way to get on Gladys Heartwood's good side, Celeste knew it. Her mother loved two things: white chocolate popcorn and a peach fritter from No Dough.

Celeste held up the bag and shook it slightly. "Two peach fritters."

"I'm so glad I haven't started making breakfast yet." Her mom smiled and accepted Celeste's hug. "How are you, baby?"

"Good," Celeste said. "Really good. Where's Grams?"

"She's in the bathroom. Dad's on the back porch."

Celeste set the pastry bag on the counter and went out

onto the porch. "Hey, Daddy." She leaned over and planted a kiss on her father's forehead.

"Hey, Celeste." He grinned at her like he was the happiest man alive because she came to visit. "You gonna sit by me?" He picked up the pillow on the other half of the loveseat, and Celeste did sit by him.

She loved her father. She'd been the second daughter to come along, and being behind the perfect Olympia had not been easy on her. They'd bickered constantly, and her mother always seemed to favor O. But her father had doted on her. Taken her for daddy-daughter dates and paid for her to get her nails done before dances and taught her how to change a tire.

Not that she actually did that—she called her father, who came and took care of whatever Celeste needed him to.

She linked her arm through his and sighed as she leaned her head against his shoulder. "It's nice here," she said. "You guys are much closer to the beach that we are."

"Yeah, there's that big swell moving north," he said. It definitely put the house Gwen and Celeste lived in farther from the actual shoreline.

"Daddy?" she asked.

"What, jitterbug?"

Celeste smiled out at the waves rolling ashore. "I met a new man."

"Ho, boy," her dad said with a chuckle. "Is he a nice

man? Because I don't think any of the others have been all that great."

"It's just the beginning," she said. "And it's a secret, okay? You can't tell anyone, even Mom."

"Yeah, all right," he said, though Celeste knew he'd tell her mother. And his. They didn't keep secrets from each other, which was why she didn't tell him who the new man was. And he didn't ask. He just sat with her, and when her mom opened the door and asked, "Celeste, do you want coffee?" he said, "I'll take some, honeybee."

Celeste loved his Southern drawl. She loved how easygoing he was, though he hadn't always been like that. He'd run the inn before turning everything over to Olympia almost a year ago, and she remembered him leaving the house in suits early in the morning. She'd go to bed before he came home, but he always came in a pressed a kiss to her forehead before he went to bed.

"Yes, I'll have coffee," she told her mom, because her mom made the best coffee on the island. A few minutes later, she brought out two mugs, and Celeste sipped happily.

"Dad, I'm thinking about bringing in another act for Christmas." Before he'd trained Olympia, he'd worked with Celeste on all of their events. She'd been overseeing that arm of The Heartwood Inn for a few years now.

"Do we have room in the schedule?" he asked.

"I think we do," she said. "It wouldn't have to be long,

and it'll increase bookings right near the beginning of December, after they drop."

"You do what you think is right," he said. "Which act will come in only four months?"

"There's a really great Cirque de Soleil type of group that's local to Whistlestop Shores," she said. "Some of the hotels there have treated them badly, and I got an email from their manager yesterday. I think we should give them a try."

Because everyone deserved a chance. Her mind flew back to her proposal for Brad's non-profit, and she pulled out her phone. They'd been texting back and forth since their second date had gone so well.

He'd said he'd talked Bella "off the ledge" and "convinced her to keep quiet about the engagement for now."

They'd started a new game last night—*Did you know?*

She typed quickly, glad her father wasn't reading over her shoulder. *Did you know I once submitted a proposal to your construction company for an outdoor wedding hall?* She sent the message before she could second-guess herself.

She'd been harboring negative feelings for him since that proposal had gone unanswered, but now that she'd spent some time with him, she knew the man didn't have a mean bone in his body.

He was probably just busy at the time, like she constantly seemed to be.

I had no idea. When?

When you first started up, she said. *I wasn't happy when you won the bid for the swimming pool at Heartwood.*

I'm calling you.

I'm at my parents house.

Call me when you leave.

She tipped her phone against her body so she couldn't see the screen.

"Is that him?" her father asked. "The new man?"

"Yes."

"I could tell."

"How?" Celeste asked, looking at him.

"You sighed happily when you texted him." Her father looked at her with such kind, blue eyes. "Seems like you like him."

"You know what, Dad? I do. I really do." And those were some of the scariest words Celeste had ever said out loud.

But nothing would rival introducing him as her fiancé to her sisters at the party that weekend.

9

B rad took off his shirt and threw it on the bed, surveying the clothes already there. He felt like an idiot, because Celeste had said the dress was casual that night. But he'd been engaged twice, and he knew how important meeting the sisters was.

And for Celeste?

He better wear the exact right shirt with his charcoal slacks. He picked up the light blue one he'd had on a few minutes ago, and pulled it over his head again. Tiny pinstripes adorned the bottom third, and he decided the polo would have to do.

A moment later, knocking sounded on his front door, and he hurried down the hall and through the living room to answer it.

Celeste stood there, he own dark slacks sexy and slim-ming on her legs. She wore heels, which brought her closer to his height, and her blouse was black with a bright pink and blue floral design.

In short, she was *stunning*.

In the week since he'd run scared into her office and asked her to play pretend with him, Brad had developed some real feelings for the woman.

"You look amazing," he finally said, though she was still sizing him up. "How'd I do with the shirt?"

"It's great," she said, tiptoeing her fingers up the three buttons to his collar. Shockwaves moved through his shoulders and down his arms from her touch, and her skin hadn't even met his yet.

Their eyes met, though, and she looked like she might be sick.

"You okay?" he asked.

"Yeah," she said, stepping into his house. "Want to give me a tour? We have a few minutes."

"Sure." He closed the door behind her, glad it was Friday, as his cleaning service came on Thursday afternoons. His coffee cup still sat in the sink from that morning, but other than that, the house was quite clean.

"Living room," he said, indicating the leather couches. "Standard. Kitchen." He walked past the furniture that marked where the living room ended. "I mostly eat out." He couldn't remember the last time he'd done more than fry an egg or make a sandwich.

"Is that because you don't like to cook or don't know how?" she asked.

"I don't know how, which means I also don't like it." He smiled at her, surprised and yet thrilled when she slipped her hand into his. They weren't in public, and he had a moment where he wanted to call her on breaking her own rules.

No touching unless we're in public.

They hadn't spent much time in public after that second try at Radish, but he'd seen her around the inn, and they texted a whole lot.

They'd talked a few times, most notably when she'd called to tell him how she'd submitted a project for a grant he'd done. He'd asked her to tell him about it, but the proposal hadn't seemed familiar.

She claimed she'd never heard back, but Brad himself had made sure every submission got a response. He'd told her he'd check into hers, but she'd told him he didn't need to.

He had anyway, if only to satisfy his own curiosity. And because she'd disliked him because of her perception that he hadn't responded to her.

Brad probably would've chosen to fund her outdoor wedding hall had he seen her proposal. Number one, he loved supporting local Carter's Cove businesses, and number two, he liked partnering with other powerful people.

And whether Celeste knew it or not, the Heartwoods were powerful on the island. They owned prime beach real estate and the ritziest resort south of Whistlestop

Shores.

"I asked how many bedrooms," Celeste said, her grip on his hand tightening. "I think I lost you."

"Sorry," he said, blinking out of his memories of their conversations that week. "Uh, three bedrooms. Two bathrooms. A little deck." He pointed out the French doors. "It's no beach view, but it's nice."

"It is nice," she said. "And north side of the island. Houses up here aren't cheap."

"Did you know I played professional football for seventeen years?" he asked in a teasing tone.

She giggled and ducked her head, those soft curls falling between them. Brad reached out and tucked them back, which drew Celeste's eyes to his. Something like fairy dust descended on him, and his gaze dropped to his mouth.

He really wanted to kiss her.

Clearing his throat, he stepped back and said, "We should go."

"Yes," she agreed readily. "Yes, we should."

He swiped his keys from the kitchen counter and headed for the garage exit. "I thought we'd take the truck tonight. Is that okay?"

"Sure," she said, her voice still a little on the awkward side. What had she been thinking in that magical moment? Would she let him kiss her?

He shook the thoughts from his mind as he opened the garage door and helped Celeste into the truck. First, he had to make it through the party. Then he could think about kissing her.

They arrived at the inn several minutes later, and he went into an employee lot, as directed by Celeste. She led him in a back door, and before he knew it, they were walking toward a large table with three other blonde women.

Her sisters.

Brad swallowed and squeezed Celeste's hand. She'd given him very few instructions for tonight, and he wasn't sure why she'd suddenly stopped dictating to him what to do or how he could act.

"Oh, dear Lord in heaven," Olympia said, her eyes locking onto Brad. She stood up and tossed her napkin on the table. "Bradley Keith." She looked at Celeste, easily twenty questions swimming in those blue eyes. "Are you two...?"

Celeste held up her left hand, where the diamond could've blinded someone ten yards away. "We're engaged."

"Engaged?" at least three people said simultaneously. From there, chaos erupted. Every woman had something to say, from a statement to a question to giggling. They all ogled the ring, and everyone hugged Celeste too.

"Okay, what's going on?" another woman asked, and Brad turned to her. "I thought this was my party."

"Celeste is wearing a diamond," Olympia said. "A *huge* diamond."

Alissa—Brad assumed, as it was supposed to be a dinner celebrating her opening the fish monger shop— looked like she'd been hit with a brick. "What in the world?" She looked from Celeste to Brad.

"Hello," he said. "Hello, everyone. I'm Bradley Keith."

"*The* Bradley Keith?" Alissa asked, her eyes widening.

"You can call me Brad," he said, shifting his feet and reaching for Celeste's hand again. He didn't appreciate her leaving him out to dry like this.

"Sorry, Alissa," Celeste said. "It's nothing, really. Let's sit down. This night is about you."

But Brad knew better. This night was all about Celeste, and he suddenly felt like she was using him in the worst way possible.

"Let me introduce you," she said.

"Yes," another sister said. "Let's do introductions."

"I'll start," Olympia said, retaking her seat. Brad sat next to her, with Celeste on his right. "I'm Olympia Heartwood, and this is my boyfriend Chet Chadwick." She beamed at him, and Brad could see why. He was handsome, and with a name like Chadwick, when he bought Olympia a diamond, it wouldn't be small.

"Celeste," Celeste said. "And my...fiancé, Brad Keith."

"I'm Alissa. And this is my boyfriend Shawn Newman."

The Newman's lived on Carter's Cove too, and Brad was glad to recognize another name.

"Sheryl," the next sister said. "And my boyfriend Gage

Sanders. He's the new head baker here." She smiled at him, obviously proud.

"Gwen," the last woman said, and Brad smiled at the familiar face. "And I have no boyfriend or fiancé." She narrowed her eyes at Celeste, and Brad felt his date shiver beside him. She'd probably be up all night explaining things to her sister.

And for one brief moment, Brad thought she deserved it. He turned to Gage next to him. "So you're a baker." He didn't look like a baker, but Brad tried not to judge people before he knew them.

And yet you did exactly that to Celeste.

"I used to be a Marine," Gage said, and Brad smiled and nodded, shocked by his thoughts and glad he didn't have to talk for a minute.

Thankfully, he didn't have to talk a whole lot during dinner at all. The first course arrived, and the Heartwood sisters chitchatted with each other as if they hadn't seen each other in months.

When the event finally ended, he drove slowly back to his place, quiet and stuck inside his own thought patterns.

"You're being quiet," Celeste said.

"Nothing to say," he said, though there were plenty of words piling up beneath his tongue.

"I don't believe you."

He made the final turn onto his street. "Did you want to stay engaged to help me? Or help yourself?"

"I did say I'd like a fiancé this summer. I told you that."

"Yeah." He looked out the window, because she had said that. It didn't make him feel any less foolish though. This was a complete game to her, and he'd gone and started to like the woman.

Stupid, stupid, stupid, he told himself, the way his grandfather had done on the horse farm when Brad didn't secure a gate right, and the prime horse on his grandfather's farm had gotten out.

His grandfather had been so mad, and Brad had learned that details mattered.

He pulled right into the garage, all thoughts of kissing her completely gone now. He didn't even want to look at her. She got out of the truck herself, and Brad went up the steps that led to the house.

"Are you upset?" she asked.

He turned back to her, trying to decide if this conversation was worth having. "You know what, Celeste? Yes, I'm upset." He twisted the knob and went inside his house, leaving her in the garage.

Half of him hoped she'd just get in her car and leave. She'd wanted to come to his place, because she was already out at a florist or a dressmaker or something to do with one of her brides.

But he should've known she wouldn't just leave without talking this through. He knew her well enough to know that. He'd just tossed his keys on the counter when the door closed behind him again.

"Why are you upset?" she asked.

"You paraded me around like a piece of meat. How's that for you?" He leaned into the kitchen counter behind him and folded his arms. "How would you feel if I told you to dress up real nice and then took you to meet all of my buddies, just so I could show them how awesome I am?"

"That is not—"

"That is *exactly* what happened tonight," he said. "And if you can't see that, you're delusional."

Celeste glared at him for a few seconds, and then the fire left her eyes. "I'm sorry, Brad."

"I—what?"

"You're right."

He was not expecting her to say that, and he had nothing to add to the conversation.

"I shouldn't have done that," she said. "I'm sorry it made you feel like a piece of meat." She nodded, and he thought she really meant it.

"Okay," he said. "Thank you for apologizing."

Celeste tucked her hair behind her ear, and Brad wished he'd been the one to do it. "Are we still on for the music festival tomorrow?"

"Yes," he said. "I'm going to breakfast with my sister in the morning, too."

"Oh, that's right. You'll call me after?"

"Yep."

Celeste came into the kitchen and put one hand on his still-clenched arms. "I really am sorry."

"I know, Princess."

She cocked her head. "Why do you call me that?"

"You're kind of like a princess," he said. "All the pieces always in the exact right place." He swallowed, his throat dry. "So beautiful, all the time." He loosened his arms and let his hands fall to his side.

"Thank you," she murmured, stretching up to place a delicate kiss on his cheek.

Brad held very still as she settled back onto her heels and turned to leave. "See you tomorrow," he said from his safe position in the kitchen.

"Bye." She lifted one hand in a wave, a gorgeous smile on her face, and left through the front door.

Brad closed his eyes and breathed in deep, the scent of Celeste's perfume still hanging in the air around him. Her touch burned through his blood, and he sighed.

"You're an idiot," he said to the empty house, wishing now more than ever that he had a dog to talk to that night.

"SO YOU'RE SAYING IT'S NOT REAL," BELLA SAID, REACHING for the saltshaker.

"No," Brad said, though he'd kind of said that. "I'm saying it's not a big deal. I'm saying it might get called off, like the other two engagements I've had."

His sister frowned as she seasoned her scrambled

eggs. "I don't understand. Why would you ask her to marry you if you thought it would get called off?"

"I don't know," Brad said. "Why did my other two engagements fail?"

Bella rolled her eyes. "Come on, Brad. Really?" She speared a chunk of sausage and then a bit of egg and put it all in her mouth.

Brad sipped his coffee and looked down at his Belgian waffle. "I'm just saying this doesn't need to be a big deal. Celeste hasn't chosen a date, and she said it'll probably be a year before we get married." He'd need to text her and tell her that, just in case someone else mentioned it to her.

"Why so long?"

"She's a Heartwood," Brad said, as if that summed it up. And it kind of did. They were Southern royalty. "Her inn is booked for a solid year, in case you didn't know."

"She can't find a date for her own wedding?"

"I don't think she's looked." Brad sighed. "Are we going to talk about this the whole time?" He was tired of it already, and they'd only been in the restaurant for twenty minutes.

"No," Bella said. "What would you like to talk about instead, Mister Smarty-Pants?"

"Mister Smarty-Pants?" Brad looked at her and started laughing. She joined him, and he felt a measure of happiness that had been missing for a while.

"How are the kids?" he asked when they quieted.

"Oh, you know," Bella said. "Kids. They drive me crazy, but I love them."

"Yeah." Brad nodded. "They were good at the water park a couple of days ago."

"And it's all they've been talking about." His sister smiled at him. "Isn't Celeste a lot younger than you? Maybe you'll have some kids of your own."

Brad scoffed, because the idea of him and Celeste actually getting married and having children was so high on the ridiculous chart, he couldn't even see it up there.

At the same time, he had sudden hope that they would indeed be able to make their relationship work— and that maybe it wasn't too late for him to be a father.

10

"I don't believe you for a single second, you know," Gwen said from where she lay on Celeste's bed. "Alissa says she thinks it's real, and Olympia said she's withholding judgement." Gwen looked away from her phone, expecting Celeste to say something.

She didn't know what to say. She didn't want to admit out loud that the engagement was a farce, but she didn't want to lie either.

"You're supposed to be helping me pick my outfit for the music festival," she said, and Gwen rolled her eyes.

"Fine, be that way."

"I will be that way," Celeste said. "When you ask out Teagan, I'll tell you everything you want to know about me and Brad."

"Not you too."

"Of course me too," Celeste said. "We all saw you two last night. He may act like he's over you, but he's not."

"We never even kissed," Gwen said. "Never. I wish everyone would butt out of my business."

"Oh, you mean how you've been butting out of mine?"

"Celeste." Gwen got up and took the blouse Celeste was holding in front of her body. "You showed up with a huge diamond and a celebrity. There's a big difference there."

"You knew I was dating him."

"You went out with him on Tuesday," Gwen said. "And showed up engaged on Friday." She shook her head and rifled through the pile of clothes on the end of the bed, finally pulling out a flimsy blue top. "This."

"That?" Celeste took it and straightened it out before holding it up. "It does bring out the blue in my eyes."

"And you wear a sexy tank top under it, which he can see, and you'll make him wish this engagement were real." She looked at Celeste with cocked brows, but Celeste wasn't going to play her sister's games.

"Shoes?" she asked.

"White sandals," she said. "Not the wedges. The music festival is on uneven ground." Gwen flopped back on the bed and picked up her phone. "I would like someone to go out with."

"Maybe just try Teagan again." Celeste sat down on the bed and looked at her sister. "Sweetie, you deserve the best."

"And that's not Teagan, so I wish everyone would just leave me alone about him." Gwen looked a breath or two away from crying, so Celeste nodded.

"Okay, I will."

"Thank you."

She leaned over and hugged her sister. "Thanks for helping me be less fashion challenged."

"You'd die without me," Gwent said.

"I really would." Celeste straightened and started getting dressed. "I also think I'm going to go more natural with my makeup today."

"Wise," Gwen said. "It's about five thousand degrees out there. It'll all melt off anyway."

Celeste groaned, because if there was one thing about the music festival she didn't like, it was the heat. Oh, and all the cigarette smoke.

She did go lightly with her makeup, wondering if Brad would notice. When he knocked on the door several minutes later, she opened the door to find him wearing a casual pair of khaki shorts and a button-up shirt in a color of coral she would've never picked for him. But he looked delicious enough to eat, and Celeste grinned at him.

"Wow, don't you look nice?" he asked. "I like what you did with the makeup."

"Less is more, right?" she asked, reaching for her purse. "Ready?"

"Celeste?" he asked, and she paused on the threshold of the house. "I've been meaning to...I mean...." His eyes dropped to her mouth again, and Celeste looked at his lips too.

She'd thought about kissing him—she wasn't dead inside. "You didn't call me after breakfast with your sister," she said.

"Yeah, well," he said, shuffling his feet. "How would you feel if we skipped the music festival and just took a walk down the beach?" He extended his hand toward her.

Light filled her whole soul. "That would be lovely," she said, putting her hand in his and leaving her purse in the house.

He drove down the coastal highway, the silence between them comfortable but also very present. "Was breakfast bad?" she asked.

"Do you want kids?" he blurted out.

"Oh, wow," she said, staring at him fully now.

"My sister just said some stuff that got me thinking," he said, glancing at her. "I've always thought, well, the last few years I've thought I was too old to be a dad."

"How old are you?" Celeste asked, thinking she probably should know that about her freaking fiancé.

"Forty-seven."

"Ah. I'm a decade younger than you."

"I know, Princess." He pulled off into a parking lot on the west side of the island, a beautiful stretch of beach before them. He parked and left his shoes in the car. Celeste did the same, slipping her hand into his.

"Yeah, I want kids," she said.

"Mm." They walked through the hot, squishy sand to the harder, wetter stuff and started walking, nowhere to go and not in any hurry. A breeze came off the water, making the temperatures more bearable. Families and couples and groups of teenagers filled the sand, but the farther they went from the parking area, the less populated the beach became.

"Celeste, I have to be honest with you."

"Okay," she said, anticipation dancing through her.

"I'm not sure this fake engagement is going to work out."

Her heart beat against fear now. "Why not? I thought it was going well."

He paused and looked into the sun arcing down. Sunset was still hours off, but the sky was still beautiful. "Because I have *real* feelings for you." He looked at her, and even through their sunglasses, she could see the truth in his eyes.

"You do?"

"Yes." He swallowed. "And maybe this isn't so fake to me."

Celeste tingled from head to toe. "Maybe it's not so fake to me either."

Brad smiled, swept one arm around her waist, and leaned down. "Then I'm going to kiss you for real, okay?"

She gave a single nod, because she couldn't find the brainpower to vocalize anything. Her eyes drifted closed, and the breeze played with her hair, and finally Brad's lips touched hers. He teased. He toyed. And then he finally kissed her like he meant it, taking his time to truly kiss her.

Celeste matched him stroke for stroke, letting him know that this *definitely* wasn't fake to her.

He broke the kiss several seconds later and rested his cheek against hers. "I like you, Celeste Heartwood. Even when you make me mad, I still like you."

She held onto his broad shoulders and enjoyed breathing in and out with him. She finally said, "I like you too, Brad." She pulled back and looked into his eyes. "And not just because you're fun to parade around, though you are." She smiled at him, glad when he laughed.

She did too, grateful for his candidness and for simple things like walking on the beach.

"Yes, hello?" she said into her desk phone. Paige had connected her to the manager for The Living Waters, a woman named Judy. But their connection had been bad the first time, and Celeste had called her back.

"I can hear you now," Judy said.

"Okay, great." Celeste looked down at her calendar. "I think we'd love to host you at The Heartwood Inn," she said. "But we have a very limited window during our holiday season. How would December first through the fifth work for you?"

"We'd love that," Judy said almost before Celeste had finished speaking. "Let me just check our calendar...." A few seconds went by. "We can make that work."

"I have your fee schedule, and we'd love two shows on Saturday, the second, and Sunday, the third, which is seven shows. There's no price for seven shows." She loved planning events, and this one would fill a weekend where Heartwood didn't typically have anything. That first weekend of December was somewhat of a dead zone between Thanksgiving and the Christmas season really ramping up.

But with The Living Water—a show about the Savior and his birth, which happened to fit in with Christmas really well—on that weekend, the inn could book more rooms at a somewhat slower time.

Their tree decorating and lighting was always the weekend after Thanksgiving, and the hotel had been booked for that event for months.

"Four thousand," Judy said. "If you sell out the pool, you'll make four times that."

"I'm sorry," Celeste said. "The pool?"

"Our show involves diving and synchronized swimming," Judy said. "You have the pool facilities at Heartwood, or I wouldn't have contacted you."

"So this would be an outdoor show?"

"Yes," Judy said.

Celeste couldn't picture the show in a swimming pool.

Surely it wasn't just any old swimming pool. "And you don't need anything specific?"

"Nope."

"Maybe you'd like to come show me what you do." She clicked on her laptop, though her calendar was already up. "I have some time later this week. Wednesday? Or Thursday, but only before noon that day."

"Thursday morning would work," Judy said. "And there are a couple of links to some videos in the email I sent you."

"I'll look at those," Celeste said. "I admit I didn't."

"What made you give us a chance then?" Judy asked. "Most people only consider us after seeing the videos."

"I just had a good feeling about you," Celeste said with a smile. "I'll see you Thursday." The call ended, and she stared a new file for The Living Waters. Everything would go in the folder on her computer, and a physical one Paige would file and keep in the office. That way, nothing got missed. Payments were made on time, and contracts could be referenced if necessary.

Paige knocked and entered. "We've got the contracts for Betsy and Joe Harmon," she said, peeling off the top file folder and handing it to Celeste. "And three proposals for spring shows here at the inn. I told them they were a bit early to be sending stuff in, but here they are." She passed over the folders. "And your fiancé is waiting out here."

"He is?" Celeste tried to look past Paige, but the other woman shifted to block the view.

"No, he is not." She sat down, her dark eyes like lasers. "You're engaged, and you didn't tell me?" She actually sounded hurt, and regret lanced through Celeste.

She hadn't even told her own sister that the engagement was fake. She couldn't tell Paige and not Gwen.

"It happened very quickly," Celeste said. Not a lie.

"You don't wear a ring," Paige pointed out.

Celeste opened the top drawer in her desk and pulled out the diamond ring. Paige gasped as she passed it over, and she even slid it all the way on her finger. "This is huge."

"He's a former football player," she said, as if Paige didn't know who Brad Keith was. They'd had lunch last week, where Celeste had told Paige she was dating Brad—the same thing she'd told Gwen.

So jumping from that to engagement was a surprise. Even for her.

"Is this real?" Paige asked, and it took Celeste a moment to realize she was asking about the diamond, not the engagement.

"Of course it is." Celeste held out her hand. "Now give it back."

"I've never been engaged," Paige said wistfully.

"That's because you date losers, like I used to." Celeste put the ring back in the top drawer. "I think there's a guy who works here with Brad. Jonas?" Or was it James?

"It's James," Paige said. "And I flirted with him in the elevator last week. The man wasn't interested."

Celeste thought of Gwen and all her troubles with Teagan. "Maybe he just doesn't want you to think he's interested."

"And maybe he's *not* interested." Paige stood up. "It's fine. I'm fine. I'm going to that love-to-forty event next week."

"Oh, I'm super excited about that," Celeste said. "And you're an excellent tennis player, so *surely* you'll meet someone." She'd put together the singles event happening on the tennis courts at Heartwood next Friday night.

It was a tennis match, speed dating, and a mix-and-mingle all in one. And the name was off-the-charts cute—and she'd come up with it herself. "Which reminds me...I need to check on the food for that event."

"I already have the file out," Paige said. "And I've already called. We're set. They're delivering at six-thirty for setup and a start time of seven."

Celeste smiled at Paige. "You're awesome, you know that? You're going to find the right guy, I'm sure of it."

"I hope so." Paige sighed as the phone rang at her desk out in the lobby. She left to answer it, and Celeste couldn't help opening the top drawer of her desk and looking at the diamond ring again.

Brad was the best man she'd been out with in forever and confessing her real feelings and kissing him had opened her mind to more possibilities. Maybe he was "the right guy" for her too.

Now, all she had to do was figure out how to break-up with him—and then get back together again, *without* a fake engagement ring.

11

B rad loved walking through a construction site, and he went down the steps and into the huge pool bowl with James, who kept pointing to things and giving details about them. "The tile's in," he said. "And we should have the project done on time."

"Really?" Brad asked. "On time?" Construction projects never finished on time.

"That's right. Bill said he'd get a staff meeting together, and they'll take it from here by next week."

Brad looked around, thinking so much still needed to be done. But he had a crew of eleven employed on this site, and they worked full shifts, so the tile would go in quick. The painting would get done in a day. It really was marvelous what they could do when they had all the supplies they needed.

"Great," he said. "And then you're taking your crew over to Mount Vernon Hills, right?"

James groaned and rolled his eyes. "Can't you send Louis's crew over there? It's an hour drive after the ferry ride."

"I know, but it's a huge job," Brad said. "Eight months on the pediatric wing in the hospital."

"I know. That's why I don't want to have a three-hour commute for the next eight months. None of the guys will want that."

"Some of them live across the channel," Brad argued back. "I'll put you in a rental if you want." James didn't have a family, and he could move to Mount Vernon Hills for the job.

"Really?"

"Yeah, really. Ask and see if there's anyone else who might want to do that. You guys can be roommates."

"All right," James said. "I'll get in touch with the hospital administrator and get things rolling with that."

Brad grinned at him. "Perfect."

"What are you working on next?"

"I've got to get some more bids out," Brad said. Sometimes construction projects came to him, but if he wanted to keep his three foremen and their crews working full-time—and he did—he had to be out in the surrounding area, looking for jobs. "Donna and I are meeting this afternoon to go over some finals before she sends them out."

His other two crews were a few months from being

finished with their jobs, so Brad had some time to get on someone else's radar. His celebrity status helped, as did his excellent reviews for his company.

"And it's your parents' anniversary tonight, right?" James asked. "How's the fake fiancée?"

"Uh, good," Brad said a little too brightly.

"Uh oh." James chuckled as he went up the steps and out of the empty pool. "Doesn't sound good."

"No, it is," Brad said. "It's just...complicated." He didn't want to discuss his relationship with his employee, even though he and James were good friends.

"Meaning you started to like her for real." James laughed fully then, his voice echoing off the empty spaces in the construction site. "I thought you said she was uptight and bossy."

"Well, she is," Brad said. "But they're actually good qualities."

"She's beautiful, I'll give her that."

"And smart," Brad said. "And when she relaxes, she's actually really fun to be with." More than fun. He was excited to spend time with Celeste, and her fun, flirty texts made him smile whenever she messaged.

"I'll catch you later," he said, and he ducked out of the plastic. Since Celeste's office was literally steps down the hall, he went that way. Through the door, the scent of fresh dryer sheets filled the air, and he met eyes with the brunette behind the desk.

"Hey," he said. "Is Celeste in?" He hadn't seen her for a

couple of days, as he'd been on a job site across the channel.

"Yes, let me see if she's available." She picked up the phone and said, "Celeste, your boyfriend is here," her eyes never leaving Brad's. A few seconds passed, and she said, "Okay, sure."

She hung up and stood up. "She needs a couple of minutes. She's finishing something for a client. You can wait right there."

Brad grinned at her. "Thanks, Paige." He pointed to her nameplate on her desk. "It's Paige, right?"

She smiled right on back at him. "Right."

He moved over to the couch and sat down, a sigh leaking from his mouth. Not ten seconds later, Celeste's office door opened, and she came out, looking fantastic in a black jumpsuit that billowed around her legs and cinched her waist in to show all her feminine curves.

He jumped to his feet. "Hey, Princess," he said, feeling like someone had injected him with sunshine. "Do you have time for lunch?"

She took his face in both hands and smiled softly at him. Brad felt like they were the only two people on Earth, and he liked that she got his heart beating in a way a woman hadn't in a long time. Maybe ever.

"I think so," she said. "But can we just go to the bakery downstairs? I have a conference call in an hour."

"Sure thing," he said.

"Come in for a sec," she said. "I just need to grab my

purse." She retreated back into her office, and Brad would've gone to the moon when she looked at him with that playful edge in her eyes.

He didn't close the door, and she didn't move to get her purse. As soon as he was fully in the office, she kissed him, and Brad chuckled against her lips. "Did you miss me, Princess?" His pulse rippled like a flag in a stiff breeze, glad when she just answered by matching her mouth to his again and kissing him like she'd *definitely* missed him.

THAT NIGHT, FRESHLY SHOWERED AND SHAVED, DRESSED IN A suit, and with a bouquet of flowers for his parents, he drove to Celeste's house with the top up on his convertible. He didn't want a hair out of place for the anniversary dinner, and his nerves had his fingers clenched around the steering wheel.

Gwen answered the door, and Brad gave her a quick hug. "Good to see you, Gwen," he said. "How are things in the kitchens?"

"Hot," she said with a smile.

"I'll bet they are," he said.

"Celeste is obsessing over her earrings," she said as she retreated into the kitchen. "I told her what to wear, but she's not listening to me."

"I thought she consulted you for her fashion choices," Brad said.

"Yeah, she's nervous."

Brad glanced toward the hall that led back to the bedrooms. "Can I...?"

"Be my guest. She's dressed, and I did pick her outfit. It's marvelous," Gwen said with a laugh.

Brad could only imagine. Celeste never wore anything that didn't look absolutely amazing on her, and he wondered how much her clothes cost. They looked expensive, and when she put all the pieces in the right place—makeup, jewelry, shoes, handbag—she looked like a million bucks.

Of course, Brad liked it when she just wore jeans too, and he really wanted to see her in sweats and a T-shirt, maybe doing some gardening or something that got her hands dirty and sweat beading along her forehead. Yeah, that would be sexy to him too.

She stood in front of her dresser, looking in the mirror. "Hey," he said. "The earrings don't really matter, Princess."

"Oh." She jumped and pressed one palm to her heartbeat. "You scared me."

"I rang the doorbell and everything."

"Come help me."

He entered her bedroom, noting that her bed was indeed made with crisp lines. A stack of books littered her nightstand, as did a tablet and her charging cables.

Jewelry and makeup was strewn across the dresser, and she lifted a large pair of double hoops to her ears.

"These?" She set them down and picked up some teardrop-shaped dangly earrings. "Or these?"

"Those," he said, because he honestly did not care. His mother wouldn't either. No one but her would.

"Gwen said these too," she said. "They must be the pair." She started to put them in, and Brad couldn't help leaning over and touching his mouth to her neck.

She stilled, and Brad looked at her in the mirror. So much was said without a single word being vocalized, and he took the earrings from her and slipped the first one through the hole in her lobe. "You're gorgeous," he whispered just before pressing a kiss right behind the earring he'd just put in.

She held very still as he moved behind her to do the other side. He secured that earring for her and slid his arms around her, pulling her back into his body. "I want to talk about breaking up."

"You do?" She looked absolutely terrified, and he watched her neck move as she swallowed.

"Yeah," he said, not caring if she knew how he felt. Surely she could feel it every time they kissed. "Because I want to really be who Paige said I was earlier today."

"What did she say?" Celeste asked.

"She said I was your boyfriend," he said. "Not a fake fiancé." James's words rang in his ears, and he hated that they were there, complicating everything. "Not even a fiancé, actually." He quirked one eyebrow. "You didn't tell her?"

"I didn't, but she found out."

"She thinks it's real?"

"Everyone thinks it's real," Celeste whispered. "I haven't even told Gwen that it's not."

"Hmm." Brad dipped his head and kissed the spot where her shoulder met her neck, and she leaned into the touch.

"We're going to be late."

"We're fine," he murmured, enjoying the silky texture of her skin, the way she held onto his hands, the swaying as she moved closer to him and then pulled away.

Brad finally got control of himself and took a step back. "My mother will love your dress," he said.

"Yeah?" Celeste looked down at the little black number, and Brad scanned her too.

"Maybe not as much as me, but yeah." Brad chuckled, her sexy, red heels the perfect cherry on her outfit.

"Okay." Celeste took a deep breath. "I'm ready."

"Of course you are." She could do anything, and Brad really liked that. He liked that she was strong, and smart, and sexy all in one package. He offered her his arm, and they walked down the hall together.

"Bye, Gwenny," she said, though her sister was on the phone. "See you tomorrow."

"Uh, Celeste." She moved the phone away from her ear, and Brad could see that it was actually Celeste's phone. "It's Paige. There's a problem with the love-to-forty event tomorrow."

"What?" Celeste released his arm and clicked her way over to her sister. "Paige, what's going on?"

Brad's anxiety spiked, because he had a very real feeling that he would be going to his parents' anniversary party without Celeste. She turned away from him and asked another question, and his hopes for the night crashed and burned.

Celeste was strong, and smart, and sexy. But maybe she was also already married to her job, and Brad should know—he'd been accused of such a thing in the past too.

Unwilling to just leave without her, he sat on the couch and pulled out his phone. *Running late,* he texted his mother. *We'll have to meet you at the restaurant.*

Okay, Bella just got here. We'll see you there.

Brad's heart thrashed in his chest as Celeste continued to speak to her assistant. Gwen came over and offered him a bottle of water, and alarmed, Brad took it.

How long was he going to have to wait?

12

C eleste could not believe what Paige was saying. She had over one hundred people signed up for the singles event the following evening. It was less than twenty-four hours away.

"No food," she repeated. "I thought you called and confirmed."

"I did," Paige said. "And I did again just now, and they said I'm not on their delivery route."

"Can we pick it up?" Celeste asked. She'd go herself if she had to, though it was a ferry ride away, and she couldn't imagine trying to get appetizers, salads, sandwiches, and drinks back across the channel by herself. "I'll rent the freaking ferry if I have to."

"They're closing early for something," Paige said. "The food has to be picked up by three."

"Three?" Celeste sighed in heavy frustration. She

glanced over her shoulder to find Brad had sank onto the couch and Gwen was offering him a drink. "Why didn't they tell us they had to close early?"

"I guess the owner's mother died," Paige said, and Celeste felt like a real jerk.

"Oh, okay. Okay." She ran her hand through her hair, immediately regretting it. She'd spent a long time on her hair in preparation for this dinner. "It's fine. We'll pick up at three. I'll talk to the kitchen about storing the food in the refrigerator."

"This is why we should've just hired it out to our own staff," Paige said.

"They have two banquets tomorrow," Celeste said. They'd been over all of this. Yes, The Heartwood Inn almost always catered their own events. But not when the schedule was so full they couldn't.

Celeste had been using The Smoking Apple for years in instances like this, and she knew Livvy, the owner. She couldn't imagine losing her mother, and Celeste's heart went out to her.

"Okay, this is okay," Celeste said. "We'll get the food and it'll be fine."

"You have Teri Easton coming tomorrow afternoon."

"Reschedule her."

"We've already rescheduled her once."

"I don't care," Celeste said, her patience wearing thin. They were already late to Brad's dinner, and she had to go. "I have to go, Paige. Reschedule her." She hung up the phone, feeling like a complete witch. She didn't talk to Paige like that. They worked well together, because they respected each other. If she'd had more time, she'd have gone back into the office—where Paige obviously still was —and help her take care of things.

"I'm so sorry," she said, hurrying into the living room. "Let's go."

"Everything okay?" Brad asked as he stood.

Celeste felt like crying, but she would not ruin her makeup. Not tonight. "No, but I'm ready." She flashed him a tight smile, knowing she wouldn't be able to truly relax tonight during his family's celebration. "Honestly, I am. We're late. Let's go."

Brad led her outside, and she was relieved to see the top up on the convertible. He didn't say much on the way to the restaurant, and she was surprised to find him pulling into the circle drive for the valet at the inn.

"We're eating here?"

"Redfin," he said. "It's my mother's favorite restaurant."

"You're kidding." Celeste smiled, thinking maybe this night wasn't completely ruined and that maybe the gift she'd put together last minute for his parents would be a big hit. "Okay, your sister is Bella. Her husband's name is Greg, but he won't be here tonight because he's deployed overseas. Mom and Dad are TJ and Christy. And your brother David is here from Kentucky, with his wife, Jane."

"That's right," Brad said. "You're going to be fine."

She glanced down at the diamond on her finger, half-wishing it wasn't there. She drew in a deep breath and got out of the car when the valet opened her door. Brad appeared at her side, and they walked into the inn together. She rarely used the front entrance to get to her office, and she appreciated the beauty in the inn.

A huge fireplace sat opposite of the check-in desk, where three people stood ready and willing to help. The scent of salt and flowers filled the air, and a huge TV screen showed the picturesque beauty of the private beaches one could only access as a guest at the hotel.

Comfortable couches filled the space behind the fireplace, which was two-sided, and Olympia had a big sign announcing their wine tasting that evening. She and Brad went past that, and around the corner to Redfin.

"Good evening, Celeste," the host said. "Did you have a reservation?"

"We're with my family," Brad said, and the man's eyes widened.

"Oh, the Keiths. Of course. They said you'd be coming. Right this way." He started to lead them past the podium and into the restaurant. It wasn't nearly as dark as Radish —they weren't a club or trying to be terribly ritzy. They were full most evenings, no matter the day of the week, but the huge wall of windows that looked out onto the beach and the ocean let in plenty of light.

She spotted a man that bore a striking resemblance to Brad, and her pulse picked up speed.

"There they are," Brad said almost under his breath,

and Celeste shivered at the memory of that voice telling her she was gorgeous as he kissed her neck. She put a smile on her face and gripped his arm tighter.

"Hey, everyone," Brad said in a cheery voice. "David." He laughed as his brother stood from the booth and embraced him. Celeste smiled around at everyone, noting that they had all slid their gazes from the brotherly reunion to her.

"It's so good to see you," Brad said. "How's the farm? I really need to come visit."

"You so do," David said. "It's good. Really good." He looked at Celeste, and Brad molded himself right back to her side.

"This is my fiancée, Celeste Heartwood. Her family owns the inn."

Technically, Celeste owned nineteen percent of the inn, but she hadn't told Brad that and didn't need to correct him in front of his family. "Hello," she said. "It's so nice to meet all of you." She gave David a quick hug, and then his wife, who wore her dark hair short in a stylish pixie cut.

With the booth situation, she didn't get to embrace everyone, and Brad's gentle pressure on her back told her to slide in and get comfortable. She did, and he settled on the end beside her, his long legs barely fitting under the table.

"We've only ordered drinks," his mother said.

"Oh," Celeste said, reaching into her purse. "We got

you a gift. Happy anniversary." She extended the small package toward his mother, whose surprise wasn't hard to see. She didn't immediately reach for the present either.

She glanced at Brad and then his brother. "Did you guys already do gifts?"

"Celeste," Brad said, but his mother jumped in with, "Thank you, dear," and she took the gift. She opened it, which wasn't hard, as it was just a box with a silver bow around it. She peered into the box and glanced at her husband. "Oh, this is lovely," she said, pulling out the gift certificate to Redfin.

"We can come back for date night," TJ said. "Thank you, Celeste."

Brad's hand on her leg felt heavy, but she smiled and looked up at the waiter when he arrived. "Would you two like drinks? And are we ready for appetizers?"

"She'll have the strawberry lemonade," Brad said. "And I'll take seltzer water with a lot of lime."

"And yes, we're ready for appetizers," his mother said, rattling off three of them without looking at the menu.

The waiter nodded and moved to the next table, and Celeste was still aware of the awkward silence at this one.

"What do you do here at the inn, Celeste?" Bella asked.

"I manage all of the events," she said. "The big shows, the special series. The weddings."

"Sounds stressful," Bella said with a kind smile.

"It has its moments," Celeste said, covering Brad's

hand on her leg with hers. She leaned further into him, almost desperate for him to say something.

"The pool here will be done next week," he said. "Then my crew is moving over to Mount Vernon Hills."

"That's great," his mother said. "We took the Cove grandkids to the best movie today." And the conversation picked up, with everyone participating. Celeste basked in their family's vibes, finally relaxing enough to enjoy her lemonade and the delicious bacon-wrapped sea scallops that came out as the first round of appetizers.

She liked Bella, and was glad she had plenty to say. Brad's parents weren't afraid of talking either, and they seemed genuinely happy. Whatever she'd done wrong with the gift was forgotten, and they ended the evening with the cheesecake bites, which she knew were Gwen's creation.

"My sister came up with these," she said, surveying the platter of tiny two-inch square cheesecake morsels. Some had lemon curd on top, some had a glazed strawberry, some had homemade raspberry preserves, and some had peaches from just across the channel.

"The peaches come from our groves in Savannah."

"You have peach groves in Savannah?" Brad asked.

"Well, the inn owns them," she said. "But yes. And Alissa used to make the most divine peach pecan pie."

"We've had that," Christy said. "It is divine. Does she not make it anymore?"

"Well, she just opened the fishmonger shop on Main

Street," Celeste explained. "And we hired a new head baker. I'm sure he'll use the same recipe." She smiled, because this date was light years better than her first with Brad.

They said goodbye, with more choruses of happy anniversary, and Celeste practically floated out of the inn with Brad on her arm. Pure happiness filled her, and she turned toward him the moment they were alone in the car.

"That was amazing," she said. "They're so great. I mean, so great. You know that, right?"

He chuckled. "Yeah, they're not bad."

"What did I do wrong with the gift?" she asked.

"It was my fault," he said. "I should've told you we don't do gifts."

"Oh, no." Horror moved through her. "So I was the only one who brought a gift."

"It was from both of us, right?" he said. "So technically, no. You're not the only one who brought a gift."

"I'm sorry," she said. "It was a party, and I just thought...."

"It's fine, Princess," he said. "I should've told you. I forget how thoughtful you are."

She turned to look at him, marveling at how...good he was. "Did you like playing football?" she asked.

"Oh, yeah," he said. "It was a great career."

"Do you miss it?"

"Honestly?"

"Yeah, honestly."

"I miss certain aspects of it. The team, for one. I don't miss the intense workouts. I'm old now, you know?" He gave a light laugh. "My bones hurt in the morning sometimes."

"I have a gel for that," she said. "I use it on my feet. Heels can be a killer."

"I can't even imagine," he said, turning into her driveway. He put the car in park and looked at her. "That was a pretty great night, wasn't it?"

"Yes," she said. "Really great. And now I'd like to break-up with you."

His smile slipped. "What?"

Celeste giggled and opened her door to get out of the car. Brad joined her and walked her up to the front door. "You started it with the break-up talk," she said.

He put one hand on the door behind her and bent his head toward her. "I did, didn't I?"

"Yes," she said, her voice made of little more than air.

He kissed her, and Celeste had never felt such passion from a man. He kissed her so completely, a few seconds passed before she realized he'd pulled back.

"So how are we going to do that?" he asked. "It hasn't been very long."

She pressed her lips together to try to tame the tingling. "I don't know." Her fingers fumbled for the doorknob behind her, and she twisted to open the door. "You want to come in for a few minutes? Have some coffee?"

"Will we wake Gwen?"

"Not with what I have in mind," she said with a flirtatious smile. She backed into the house.

"What do you have in mind?" Brad asked, not committing to come in yet.

"Maybe some more kissing," she said. "Some talk about how we're going to break-up."

"I like both of those," he said, stepping inside. Celeste giggled as she closed the door behind him, but he cut that sound off with another passionate kiss that left her head spinning and her heartbeat racing.

She could not imagine a more perfect night, and she curled into Brad's side once the coffee was done, happier than she'd ever been.

13

B rad wouldn't see Celeste again until Sunday, as she had an onsite event for singles at the inn on Friday and Saturday. She'd invited him to come hang out with her, but he knew she'd be running around to ensure every little detail was exactly right. So he'd declined, and instead, he'd visited with his brother and his nieces and nephews.

"Uncle Brad, throw me the ball." Brad focused on his nephew Thomas and threw him the water-logged football.

"I'm going to get out, bud," he said, making his way toward the side of the pool. It was probably time to reapply sunscreen, and he really needed something to eat. He groaned as he sat in the low, beach-side chair beside his father, who looked up from his phone.

"Celeste seems very nice," his father said.

"She is very nice," Brad said, anticipating the next question his father would ask. After all, his mother had already texted him a couple of times since Thursday's dinner. It was much easier to ignore a text, though.

"You seem to genuinely like her," his dad said.

"I do."

"When did you get engaged?"

"Last week," Brad said. "I kept it out of the headlines, because I don't need that headache."

"Your mother and I are way below the headlines."

"I should've told you," he said, hoping that would be the end of it.

"I'm just going to ask once," his dad said. "Is this a real engagement? Should your mother really clear some space in her calendar?"

"There's no date set yet," Brad said, which was true. "She doesn't need to do anything. I don't need money. Celeste and I will take care of everything." He settled his sunglasses on his face and watched his brother throw the ball to his son.

Brad couldn't relax, though, even though he forced a chuckle out of his mouth while his youngest nephew did a cannonball that drenched David. He reached over and opened the cooler, pulling out one of his mother's famous ham sandwiches.

"Hey, baby," his mother said, coming over with Bella's

kids. They all picked up towels, and she handed out sandwiches. "You got one?"

"Yeah, thanks, Mom." Brad did enjoy spending time with his family, and he couldn't help how his mind went down a road he'd thought was blocked for him. One where he got to throw a ball to his own son, or watch his own daughter do a flip off the diving board.

His talk with Celeste on Thursday night about breaking up had yielded nothing. Of course, there had been more kissing than talking, and neither of them had any ideas for how to break up.

It shouldn't be that hard. It wasn't like they went to lunch with friends or needed to make a big deal of it. He could just show up at Bella's one day to pick up the kids for a fun outing and tell her, "Hey, Celeste and I broke up."

She'd take care of the rest, sending texts and making sure everyone who even got close to asking knew. At least that was what she'd done the last two times. Brad had actually appreciated it, because then he didn't have to explain anything.

"Where's Celeste today?" his mom asked as she sat beside him, her own sandwich already unwrapped.

"She has a big event at the inn," he said. "I put that in the family text."

"Oh, I must have missed it."

His mother hadn't missed it, and Brad knew it. He was

suddenly weary of being at the waterpark, but they'd only been there for a couple of hours. He could make something up, get out of there, and enjoy an afternoon on a beach somewhere. Maybe he'd even go rent a puppy for the afternoon and watch the little canine try to chase a ball through the sand.

He held onto those thoughts as everyone gathered for lunch. Thankfully, the nieces and nephews dominated everyone's attention, and Brad was able to just listen and watch and not actually participate in the conversation.

SUNDAY CAME, AND BRAD RAN DOWN THE BEACH AS THE SUN breathed new life into the day. His breathing was even, and cleansing, and he loved running when the beach was empty. He didn't work out as much as he used to when he was playing football, but enough to stay in shape. Enough to keep his mind aligned.

His phone buzzed while he ran, but he ignored it until he got home. With his chest heaving back in his own kitchen, he filled a glass with the coldest water he could get from the tap while he checked his phone.

Bella had texted three times and called twice. He frowned, his muscles starting to twitch. He moved into a lunge as he dialed his sister, surprised she was up so early. Maybe something had happened with one of the kids.

"Hey," he said. "What's—?"

"Do you get the paper?" she asked. "Not like a national one. But The Island Weekly?"

"No," Brad said. "Why?"

"You're in it today, and it is *not* good."

Brad's heart kicked into overdrive again, and he felt like running again though he'd just covered five miles.

"I'm taking pictures and sending them to you," she said. "You're not going to like it, and when Celeste sees it... well, let's just sake the fake engagement will be off."

"What are you talking about?" he asked. "Can I see it online?" Even if he could, it might take forever to read it.

"I doubt it," she said. "But you really pissed off Carmen Lunt."

Brad's heart dropped all the way to his feet and stayed there. "Carmen Lunt?"

"I'm sending them now," she said, her voice echoing, which indicated she'd put him on speaker. "They're going through. I'm sorry, Brad. Let me know what I can do to help you." She hung up, and Brad dashed over to his computer anyway.

He tapped and typed, but his phone chimed before the site would load, and his sister's pictures came in.

The headline screamed at him, making his ears ring and his knees weak.

Former football star and local hero labels fake fiancée uptight

He blinked, and the letters rearranged themselves just like they always did. Didn't matter. He'd already read the headline. Blackness edged in on his vision.

Brad shook his head, but he felt only moments away from passing out, the way he had when he'd been hit hard by a lineman in Buffalo.

He drew in a long breath, held it, and exhaled. One more breath, and he was able to look at the next picture. Carmen detailed their date, and then how he'd told her that he was engaged. *It was only when I'd confronted him the following day at work that the name of his fiancée had come out.*

I was suspicious, naturally, the article read. *He'd been out with me mere days earlier, and though he made it seem like it was just friendly, something he was doing for a friend, why would an engaged man do that?*

So I started looking into their relationship. A source finally revealed that the engagement was fake, though I will say that both Mister Keith and Miss Heartwood seem convinced themselves that they are engaged.

Brad's heart pounded. Who was her source? Besides himself and Celeste, no one else knew that the engagement wasn't real. Celeste had sworn she hadn't told anyone, not even Gwen.

And he hadn't told anyone but—"James."

James knew, but Brad couldn't believe that his best friend and foreman would say anything to Carmen, even if they were neighbors. Why would he do that?

He swiped to the next photo and started reading. *When I heard he called Miss Heartwood uptight and bossy— his fiancée. The woman he loved!—I knew I needed to print something to warn all the other females on Carter's Cove about this guy.*

Brad couldn't read anymore. He closed his eyes, willing the text to go away, but it remained etched on the backs of his eyelids.

Foolishness filled him, and he spun in a circle. He had to get to Celeste. Now. Not bothering to shower, he grabbed his keys and headed for the garage. He only lived ten minutes from Celeste's house, but it seemed to take forever to get there. Her car sat in the driveway, as it was still quite early, and if Celeste went into the office on weekends, it was always later in the afternoon.

He jogged up the sidewalk, every cell in his body rioting. "Celeste," he said, knocking loudly on the door. "Come on," he muttered. He had to talk to her before she read this article. He looked around at his feet. No paper.

And it wasn't online. Maybe he'd gotten here fast enough.

He knocked again, calling, "Celeste, please answer the door." He heard something bump inside the house, and then her dog barked a couple of times. "Midnight," he said, though the tiny poodle couldn't open the door.

Feeling frantic, he knocked one more time, glad when he heard footsteps coming toward the door. Celeste opened it, and Brad finally got the vision of her he'd been dreaming of. She wore no jewelry. No makeup. Her hair hung in limp waves on either side of her face, and she tugged her robe tighter around her, those beautiful eyes blazing.

"What are you doing here?" she asked, lifting her chin in defiance.

"She didn't say everything I said," he said, not quite sure what he was saying.

"What are you talking about?" Her phone chimed and she looked down at it. "It's so early. Why is everyone...?" Her voice trailed off, and horror washed through Brad as it flowed across her face.

"You called me uptight and bossy?"

"And then I said those were really good qualities," he said. "She didn't quote me right. And I have no idea how she found out."

Her phone buzzed and buzzed some more. She tossed it onto the side table and glared at him. "I think you should leave."

"Please, Celeste," he said. "I was talking to James at the construction site. I don't know how she overheard. But I said you were really fun to be with, and that I really enjoyed spending time with you, and that while sometimes you're a little uptight and a little bossy, it makes you really good at your job."

She folded her arms, lasers shooting from her eyes now. "I don't want to talk to you right now."

"Celeste."

"I'll call you later." She scooped up her little dog and started to close the door.

Brad couldn't very well step into the doorway and stop her from shutting him out. The door came between them, and he felt like throwing up.

14

Celeste leaned into the closed door, very aware of the sound of Brad's breathing on the other side of the door. She couldn't physically hear it, but she somehow knew he hadn't left.

So she did, moving quickly into the kitchen where she could get some coffee. Gwen hadn't left for work very long ago, and though the coffee pot as off, the brew was still warm.

Celeste didn't bother to heat it up again before pouring herself a mug. She poured hazelnut cream into the cup and added a spoonful of sugar before lifting a shaking hand to her mouth.

Tears pricked her eyes, Gwen's text burned in her brain. *There's an article in the paper where Brad calls you uptight and bossy.*

That single sentence wouldn't have made sense if Brad

hadn't been standing on her front porch, frantic to explain.

"You don't want to see it," she told herself. Gwen had deliberately not told her which paper, and Celeste knew the omission was deliberate. She took a sip of her coffee, but the taste she normally loved tasted bitter in her mouth.

She dumped it down the drain and dialed her sister. "Celeste," Gwen said, bypassing hello. "Did you get my text?"

"Yes," Celeste said, her voice so tight and so high-pitched. "I don't understand. Brad and I were getting along so great." She wouldn't cry. Not over a relationship that had started out fake and had barely been going for two weeks.

She sure did like Brad, though. She'd liked spending time with him. Liked talking to him. Liked learning that while he'd lived a high-profile life, he was down-to-Earth and human. Liked his family, and how close he was with them.

"I'm coming home," Gwen said.

"You don't need to do that," Celeste said. "The Sunday brunch is busy."

"Teagan can handle it, and I'm tired of arguing with him anyway," Gwen said. "I'm getting us tiger tails from the bakery. Do you want an orange juice?"

"Yes, and one of those red grapefruit cups."

"Be home in fifteen minutes," Gwen said. "Don't read the article, Celeste."

Celeste hung up, and she only needed five minutes to power up her laptop and search for the article Gwen had read. It was a three-minute read, and it left Celeste feeling sick to her stomach.

She put her head in her hands and wept, deciding a slow trickle of tears didn't count as crying. At her feet, Midnight whined, and Celeste picked up the little dog and took her out onto the back porch. The waves continued to roll ashore in the distance, and Celeste liked their consistency. The way they never gave up.

She'd just tapped out a message to Brad when Gwen entered the house. "Celeste? Where are you?"

"Back porch," she called, tapping to send the text before her sister could stop her. *Why would you say that about me?*

She didn't report everything I said, Brad's text came back as Gwen stepped onto the porch, pastry bags and drinks in hand. "Here you go, sweetie," she said, and Celeste shoved her phone under her thigh.

"Thanks." Celeste took her pastry and her fruit but opened her juice first. Maybe if she got her blood sugar back where it belonged, she could think clearly. Several swallows in, and she didn't feel any different.

"You read the article, didn't you?" Gwen asked.

"Yes."

Her sister sighed, but Celeste wasn't going to apologize. "Maybe he's right."

"He's not right," Gwent said.

"I am bossy," Celeste said.

"Paige doesn't think that," Gwen said. "And neither do I."

"Olympia does."

"Oh, Olympia," Gwen said, as if their oldest sister's opinion didn't matter. "You two have butted heads for so long, you'll always think she's grandstanding and she'll always think you're being bossy." Gwen shook her head with a light laugh and bit into her doughnut.

"Do you think it was her?"

"That talked to Carmen Lunt? Why would she do that?"

"Maybe she was talking to Brad, and Carmen overheard?"

"That makes no sense," Gwen said. "Why would Brad and Olympia be talking at all?" Gwen's gaze on the side of Celeste's face felt so heavy.

"What?" Celeste said, finally looking at her sister.

"The engagement was fake?"

Celeste shrugged, because she didn't want to say it out loud. Ridiculous, because everything with Brad had just been blown wide open anyway. There were no rules anymore. No reason to try not to lie.

"You didn't even tell me that," Gwen said, her voice a bit stung. "So why would Brad tell Olympia that?"

Celeste nodded, because her sister's logic was sound. "You're right." She didn't know who Brad had told. According to him, he hadn't told anyone.

Under her leg, her phone buzzed. Gwen picked up her phone, and then looked at Celeste. "It's not me."

"I don't care who it is," Celeste said. "I'm so tired of getting texts at six in the morning."

"It's almost seven," Gwen said, and that somehow made Celeste smile. And then laugh. She ate her fruit, and then her doughnut, ignoring the half-dozen messages as they kept coming in.

"What do you think I should do?" she asked.

"I'm sure all those texts are from Brad," Gwen said, groaning as she got up. "You should probably talk to him." She gave Gwen a pointed look and picked up one of Midnight's favorite balls. "I'll take your dog down to the beach."

Celeste smiled at her, a rush of gratitude and love for her sister overwhelming her. Gwen was such a good woman, and Celeste loved sharing a house and a life with her. But she wasn't a husband, and Celeste did want one of those.

As recently as last night, she'd been considering Brad for the job. "Stupid," she told herself, as they really hadn't known each other long. But sometimes the heart knew what it wanted, didn't it?

"Your life isn't a romance novel," she told herself,

finally pulling her phone out from underneath her leg. Brad had indeed texted several times.

She didn't report everything I said.

I was talking to James at the inn. Carmen must've snuck in —which really makes me mad. That's my construction site.

I also said that you have amazing qualities, and that I wanted things to be real with you.

Please, Celeste. Talk to me.

Several minutes passed before his last message had come in. *You know where to find me. I'm so sorry. I know you hate publicity.*

And she did. And the fact that he knew she did said a lot.

But what, she wasn't sure.

LATER THAT DAY, CELESTE OPENED HER TOP DESK DRAWER and dropped Brad's engagement ring inside. She'd spent more than a healthy amount of time that morning staring at it, oscillating between throwing it in the ocean and wearing it for the world to see.

As it had happened, she'd tucked it into her pocket and brought it work, just like she'd been doing for a couple of weeks now.

Brad would not be on-site today, as he actually took weekends off. But Celeste had a fiftieth wedding anniversary party that evening, and the couple didn't know about it. Their children had come in and booked the small banquet room, worked with Celeste on the menu, the décor, and the timing.

Weekends were her busiest times for events, and she really should take a couple of days off during the week. But she never did. She hadn't come to work until after noon today, and she honestly didn't mind, because she loved her job.

She closed the drawer as Paige entered the office, dressed and dolled up as professionally as ever. "Hey," she said, barely glancing up from her stack of folders. "The napkins are here, and you said to let you know when they arrived." She shuffled something. "The champagne is being chilled, and I just checked with the kitchen, and we're on schedule for the first small plates."

"Thank you, Paige," Celeste said. Her assistant started to leave, and Celeste asked, "Paige, do you think I'm uptight?"

Paige dropped all of her folders, sending papers everywhere. She didn't even try to pick them up as she turned to face Celeste. "Of course not."

"Really?"

"You're exceptionally good at your job," Paige said. "You're detailed, not uptight. Smart, not bossy. Beautiful, and talented, and if that meathead can't see it, that's his problem."

Celeste's tears sprang right back to her eyes, and she hurried around her desk to hug the best friend she had that didn't share her family name. "You're all of those things too," she said. "I apologize for anything I might have done over the years to make your life harder."

"Celeste." Paige gripped her tight. "You don't have a single thing to apologize for. I've loved working for you, and you're my best friend."

Celeste stepped back and tucked her hair behind her ears. She hadn't spent nearly the same amount of time on it as she usually did, but it didn't matter. "I'll take care of the napkins, and if you need me, I'll be down in the banquet room."

"I'm off tomorrow," Paige said. "Remember?"

"Yes, you're going to your sister-in-law's for a few days. Baby shower." Celeste turned and walked backward, a real feat in high heels. "Have fun."

"Oh, the only single woman at a baby shower. There will be no fun involved."

Celeste laughed with her friend, reassured that she hadn't treated anyone badly. She hadn't lied to anyone, not really. *She* had no reason not to hold her head high.

As she waited for the elevator, she pulled out her phone. Her fingers flew across the screen, almost faster than her mind could work. She read over the message as the elevator dinged.

Without second guessing herself, she sent it and stepped into the car, ready to be done thinking about Brad.

15

We've been looking for a way to end things, and this feels like a good way. Please come to my office to get your ring back at your earliest convenience.

Brad stared at Celeste's text, wishing the air didn't whoosh out of his lungs because of the words. They were just words, but they *hurt* more than any others he'd ever read or ever heard.

Is this a real break-up or a fake one? he texted.

Real, Brad. Her response felt clinical, and Brad didn't like that. But there was very little he liked about today. After going to Celeste's he'd gone home and showered. Sat on the couch for a while.

His stomach grumbled, which meant he hadn't eaten. He didn't really keep food in the house, so he grabbed his keys and headed out. The inn had food, and bonus, he could get his diamond ring back.

The last thought was made of sarcasm, and Brad's anger multiplied as he drove to The Heartwood Inn. The resort was magnificent, and Brad sat in his truck and breathed in deeply, appreciating how every flower bed was immaculate. The land held a sense of peace, and while it was hundreds of acres of pools and tennis courts and beaches, it still possessed a family feel.

He got out of his truck and gave the keys to the valet. "Hey, you're Bradley Keith," the kid said, and Brad nodded, his public relations smile coming right to his face.

"That's right," he said, walking away before any more questions could be asked. Surely The Island Weekly didn't have a huge circulation, but Brad felt like everyone had their eyes on him.

He got a table at Redfin, which was surprisingly busy for mid-afternoon, and he spent a long time over appetizers and Coke, a meal and dessert. When he finally couldn't stay any longer because the dinner crowd was arriving, he went up to Celeste's office. He didn't have to check with her to know if she'd be there. She usually came in on Sunday afternoons, especially if she had an event that night. And he knew she had an anniversary party that evening.

He stepped off the elevator on the second floor, his eyes going right to his construction site. He bypassed it in favor of Celeste's office down the hall, and one step into the refreshing room had regret choking him.

"Afternoon, Paige," he said when the woman didn't look up from her desk. She still didn't, and Brad took a few steps closer only to find she was asleep. Moving quietly now, he advanced to Celeste's door, almost hoping she wouldn't be there. Why he'd want to torture himself by coming here again, he wasn't sure.

Of course, he'd have to come to this floor again, as his build wasn't completed yet. Thankfully, he didn't have to deal with Celeste on the construction. He'd only seen her a handful of times in the few months he and his crew had been working to get the VIP pool built. He could avoid her for another week or two.

"Hey." Celeste stood from behind her desk, and she was an absolute vision. Brad's heart pulsed out several rapid beats and then stalled altogether.

"Hey," he managed to say.

She opened her drawer and pulled out his ring. She walked toward him, because Brad couldn't seem to move.

He took the ring from her, looking at it for several long seconds. "I'm really sorry," he said.

"I didn't mean to sound bossy when I said you should come here and get the ring," she said. "I would've brought it to you. I've just been busy this afternoon with this party."

"Celeste." He lifted his eyes to hers. "I don't think you're bossy."

"So Carmen made that up?"

"Can't opinions change?" he asked. "I mean, how

would you like your first impressions of me printed in the newspaper?"

Celeste shook her head, her emotions getting shut behind a mask. "It doesn't matter. Thank you for coming." She nodded as if she'd taken care of one more thing on her to-do list, turned, and headed back to her desk.

"That's it?" he asked.

"I really don't have anything more to say," Celeste said, situating herself behind her desk again.

A band of tension settled around Brad's chest, and he didn't know what to say either. He didn't want to leave. He couldn't stay.

He backed out of the room, wishing she'd call him back. She didn't.

Brad spent Monday at The Heartwood Inn asking his crew if they'd seen Carmen around the site in the last week. No one had.

He spent Tuesday at another build site, unfocused and out of sorts. He didn't go to work on Wednesday and instead, dropped by Bella's house, expecting her to talk his ear off.

"There you are," she said, grabbing onto his collar and dragging him into the house. She peered left and right before closing the door. "What took you so long to come by?"

"Embarrassment?" he offered. "Humiliation? The fact that I don't want to admit that I screwed up?"

"So you did have a fake fiancée," Bella said, not really asking. "And you called her bossy and uptight."

"I said that to a close friend," Brad said, already tired of explaining it. "And immediately afterward, I said she was fun to be with, and she used her somewhat unsavory qualities to be really good at her job. I said she was smart. I said—"

"I know, Brad." Bella wrapped her arms around him and held on, and Brad needed a hug more than anything. He hugged her back, closing his eyes and taking the comfort from his sister.

"So what do I do?" he asked, clearing his throat and stepping back. He put his hands in his pockets and watched his sister. "I liked her. I mean, I *like* her. I don't want to break up with her."

"I'm assuming you went and talked to her."

"Yes."

"And it didn't go well."

"No, it did not." He sighed and sat down on his sister's couch. "She gave the ring back."

"I can't believe you bought her a real ring for a fake engagement."

"It was just for a few weeks," Brad said.

"Why didn't you tell Carmen Lunt you just didn't want to go out again?"

"I did," he said. "She was relentless. Wanted to know why. I'm not good with women."

Bella sat down beside him. "That's just not true."

"Oh, it's true." Brad exhaled heavily. "Where are the kids? I want ice cream."

"It's ten o'clock in the morning."

"And I've been waiting all day." He gave his sister a smile, hoping it looked genuine enough.

"They're in the pool already," she said. "When's the last time you ate?"

"Diner, this morning," he said. "As usual." The problem was, he hated "as usual." He didn't want usual anymore. He wanted extraordinary, and that was Celeste Heartwood. He hadn't realized it until that very moment, but he'd started to fall in love with Celeste.

"Stay until lunch," Bella said. "I'll start making that turkey chili you love."

"It's a million degrees outside," he said. "I don't want chili."

"I'll cut up watermelon. I just got one yesterday. And I have parmesan, and you love salt and parmesan on your watermelon." She sing-songed the last couple of words, and Brad couldn't argue with her.

"I'll go grab some hot dogs," he said. "We can have a little wienie roast with the watermelon, and then I'll take the kids to get ice cream."

"Deal," Bella said, smiling. She paused and looked at

Brad. He knew what she was going to say before she said it. "You're a good man, Brad. This will blow over."

"I don't want it to blow over," he said. "I just want Celeste back."

"How were you planning to transition from a fake relationship to a real one?" she asked.

"We hadn't decided yet."

"Wait." Bella sucked in a breath and then started laughing. Brad didn't see what was so funny, but he just waited for his sister to calm down. "Wait, wait. Just wait a minute."

"What, Bella?" he asked, his exhaustion rolling over him in waves.

"You and Celeste were talking about a *real* relationship?"

"Yes," Brad said.

"So you were always planning to break off the 'engagement,' and then start a real relationship later on?"

"Yes," Brad said, watching his sister. "So what?"

"So that means you didn't have to make up a reason to break up. You got one. Now you just need to get back together with her." She looked absolutely delighted.

"Bella, I love you. You know that. But you sound insane. Before, the break up was going to be fake too. I wouldn't have actually done anything to make Celeste hate me."

"Oh, she doesn't hate you." Bella waved her hand as if Brad were crazy.

"You didn't see her on Sunday." Brad had, and she had not been receptive to him at all. "It's not going to work like it was supposed to before." No matter how hard Brad wished or prayed that it would.

He heaved himself off the couch. "Okay, I'm going out back with the kids."

"I'm going out for a couple of hours then," Bella said. "I'll get the hot dogs and stuff."

Brad saluted his sister, because he wanted to help her by taking the kids, and he didn't mind sitting with them in the backyard while she had some Bella-time.

Hours turned into days, and a weekend passed with Brad trying to pound Celeste out of his head by running on the beach. Nothing worked. Drinking too much soda couldn't get rid of her. Working fourteen hours a day couldn't make his mind stop revolving around her. Eating at her family's inn only made everything worse.

He ran, and he ran, and he ran, because then he had to focus on the next footstep, the next inhalation, the cool down, the recovery. He showered. He shaved. He went to an animal shelter on the mainland and found himself a mutt that needed a home as much as Brad needed a friend.

Joey was a little wired, but after a couple of mornings with six-mile runs, the dog settled right down.

Wednesday came again, and he took the dog over to Bella's house. "Heya, sissy." He gave her a kiss on the cheek. "I got a dog. His name is Joey."

"Joey!" His nephew came barreling toward Brad, who laughed as the dog went right up the six-year-old and started sniffing and licking. The little boy laughed and practically wrestled the dog to the ground as his sister came running over.

"Be careful with him, Tommy," Bella said. "Lizzie, get your things, okay?"

Lizzie did nothing of the sort, of course. The three-year-old giggled and tried to grab the dog's tail.

"We're not in a hurry," Brad said.

"I am." Bella looked at him with frustration in her expression, and Brad guessed it had already been a long day for her and it was barely noon.

"Then go," Brad said, and she turned to grab her purse. "Wait, I just have one question for you."

"Okay, what?" She pushed her hair out of her face, and Brad hoped she had a haircut on her schedule for that day while he took the kids. She loved getting her hair done, and she'd come back ready to be a stellar single mom again.

"I'm thinking about going to see Carmen," he said. "Just to talk to her. Get her to print the whole story."

"Oh, sweetie...I don't know."

"Celeste believed her over me," Brad said. "It's the only thing I can think of."

"Maybe she just needs more time. Then you can show up in her office and ask her out. How much time were you planning on taking between the fake break-up and the new get-together?"

"We hadn't discussed any of that yet," Brad said. "You go. See you tonight."

Bella hugged him, and said, "You're the best big brother on the island."

"You're bossy and uptight sometimes," he said. "Do you get all offended by that?"

"Oh, honey. If it was Greg saying that, then yes. I'd be like, maybe I wouldn't have to be like that if you were here to help." She laughed, but it didn't last long. "I know he's working, and I know he's where he's supposed to be. I'm just...tired."

"So go take care of you," Brad said. "I've got Lizzie and Tommy. They can even sleepover tonight if they want."

"Can we, Mom?" Lizzie asked, and Bella was already so worn down, she said, "All right. But you have to do everything Uncle Brad says, okay?"

The kids cheered, and Brad was even glad he wouldn't have to be alone that night. As the day wore on and he took his niece and nephew to dinner, he made a decision: He was going to see Carmen in the morning.

It was the only way he'd be able to get some closure to this situation.

16

"Okay," Paige said as she bustled into Celeste's office. She had three folders in her arms, and she spread them on the desktop. Celeste knew the color-coding system Paige had, and she appreciated it.

Paige would start with the red one, and the move to green, and then blue. "The Lively family reunion is in twenty-five days. We need to finalize décor, papers, and food. Teagan called up this morning, and I said we'd have all of our September events to him by this afternoon."

"All right," Celeste said. "I think the menu's already finalized for the Lively's. They wanted the Gold Tier Buffet, right?"

"Correct." Paige flipped open the red folder. "But there are three choices circled on the main dish, and *seven* on the sides."

"Let me get Martha on the phone." Celeste picked up

her desk phone and waited for Paige to slide the contact page in front of her so she could dial. Martha Lively never went far from her device, and she answered on the second ring.

"Martha, hello, dear," Celeste said, feeling pretentious and stuffy and...uptight. "It's Celeste Heartwood at the inn. We're finalizing your menu for the family reunion, and we have your original selections, but there are too many."

"Oh, right, right," Martha said. "Two main dishes, right?"

"Yes, and it looks like you've circled country fried chicken with pepper gravy, bone-in tilapia with bruschetta topping, and sliced flank steak with Hunter's sauce."

"We want the fish, since that is so delicious at the inn," she said. "And the chicken."

"Fish and chicken," Celeste said, nodding to Paige. She made quick checkmarks next to the selections.

"You get four sides," Celeste said. "You've marked seven."

"Read them to me?" Martha asked.

"Garlic mashed potatoes, honey glazed carrots, roasted tri-colored potatoes, potato au gratin, macaroni and cheese, wild rice pilaf, and seasonal vegetable medley."

"Well, the grandkids love macaroni and cheese, so we

need that. Garlic mashed potatoes. Wild rice pilaf. And... potato au gratin."

"All right." Celeste repeated the choices to Paige, and she set the paper off to the side.

"We've still got you down for the sweet tea and the pink lemonade," Celeste said, glad she had the Gold Tier Buffet memorized. "All meals come with the classic salad, rolls and butter, and you've chosen the chocolate mousse cake and paid extra for the bourbon pecan pie."

"That's right," Martha said.

"Great," Celeste said. "We're finalizing with our kitchen staff today, and your event is going to be spectacular." She smiled as she said it, though she felt very little enthusiasm for the upcoming events she needed to coordinate.

And she hated that. *Hated that* Brad had somehow stolen the joy from her work. Wasn't it enough that she couldn't enjoy a sunset anymore? That even her own dog reminded her of Brad's smile? She hadn't been able to eat eggs for breakfast in the week since they'd broken up, and she may or may not have driven by the diner that morning at a slow crawl, hoping for a glimpse of Brad through the window.

Foolishness hit her, and she blinked, trying to focus on Paige and the green folder she now had out. Families who were renting part of The Heartwood Inn's facilities for some reason were assigned a green or blue folder, depending on if they needed green space or water.

"...the altar from storage, and they're just doing the standard wedding reception finger foods."

"It would be nice if we had that outdoor wedding hall," Celeste said, and she wasn't even sure why it was suddenly in her mind.

"The south vineyard is usually booked when we tell people that's what we have," Paige said, barely glancing up. "We seem to do okay."

"Yeah." Celeste thought of the drawings she'd done for the outdoor wedding hall. Maybe she just needed to schedule another meeting with her sister, get past her inferiority complex when it came to Olympia, and propose the wedding hall again. The inn was doing plenty of business, and most of their rooms were booked the moment they became available.

Olympia didn't open rooms farther out than six months, and that allowed Celeste to get events on the calendar that could attract families, business, professional groups, and couples looking to come to Carter's Cove for their special memories.

"Okay, so they're ready," Paige said, reserving the food sheet for the Wilder wedding as well. "And lastly, we have the Cooper brothers." She sighed, and Celeste understood why.

She matched her sigh to her friend's and said, "Again? When are we going to tell them we're booked?"

"Never," Paige said with a smile. "Number one, you

used to have a crush on Doug, and number two, they pay twice the rate—in cash."

Celeste gasped as if Paige had said something scandalous. "I did not have a crush on Doug Cooper."

"Oh, honey." Paige laughed and shook her head. "So they'll be here Thursday night, and they've rented a half a dozen rooms."

"Are there more of them this year?"

"Apparently so," she said. "We have the breakfast buffet Friday morning, as well as the plated lunch poolside."

Celeste ran her hands through her hair. "And we put them over at Heartwood Harbor, didn't we?"

"Yes."

"Good." That pool was the farthest from the beachfront and the inn, and offered the most privacy for the party. The brothers were good-natured, but they were loud, and Celeste didn't want to be here at ten p.m. to police them as she had in years past.

"Dinner is on their own. And the following two days, we're serving dinner in the Starfish banquet room."

"Are their selections made?"

"Yes."

"So what do we need to finalize?" Celeste asked.

"We need to start gathering our chi."

Celeste met Paige's eyes, and they both dissolved into giggles. "It's five weeks away," Celeste said through the laughter.

"Yeah, and I started meditating this morning," Paige said. They sobered, and Paige cleared her throat. "No word from Brad?"

Celeste looked away, suddenly feeling hollow again. The feeling had crept into her heart and soul over the days, intensifying at some times worse than others. "No, he's not going to contact me."

"Why wouldn't he?"

"I told him not to, and Brad has class." Celeste exhaled and stood up. "I have to get going. My dad's waiting for me."

"All right," Paige said. "Have fun at lunch." She stayed in her seat, scrawling notes onto a page for the Cooper's pool party, and Celeste left her in her office. Whenever Celeste broke up with a man, she called her father and they went to lunch.

She needed to be reminded that there were good men in the world, and her father didn't ask her any questions about her now-failed relationship. That, and her father would do almost anything for fish and chips, and that was Celeste's go-to break-up food.

She'd put off the lunch for a week, though she wasn't sure why. She'd been craving the vinegary and salty taste of the fish for days, and she hurried outside to the drive-through, where her father waited in his car. The blessed blast of air conditioning hit her as she slid in with, "Hey, Daddy."

"Hey, baby," he drawled. "You ready?"

"Yep." She buckled her seatbelt and slid her sunglasses into place. "How was the fishing?"

"Relaxing," he said.

"I need some of that," she said.

"You don't have to work seven days a week," her dad said. "I keep telling Olympia that. She's doin' better now that she's got Chet."

Celeste pulled in a breath, because she'd done better when she had a reason to leave work too. "I know, Daddy," she said. "I like my job."

"But you need a way to relax."

"Yeah," she said. "I'm going to take tomorrow off and go to the beach." She hadn't truly decided until that moment, but it sounded like a good idea. A very good idea, with frozen drinks delivered to her reclining pool chaise. Gwen would even bring her whatever she wanted from the kitchen.

She tapped out a text to Paige about taking the day tomorrow as her dad drove past Main Street and up the coastal highway. The beach on the west side of the island wasn't as pristine as the one The Heartwood Inn bordered, but there was a strip of shacks on the sand that served some amazing food—including the fish and chips she and her father loved.

"I'm thinking I want some of that sorbet today too," she said, adjusting the vent to blow on her better.

"Jerry said they have the watermelon that you like," he said., referencing his best friend.

"Definitely getting some then." Celeste smiled at her father, and he smiled back.

"You're a good woman, Celeste."

Her chest pinched, and she didn't know how to answer. She looked away and tried to swallow the raging emotions rising through her throat. "Thanks, Dad," she finally said, and he started talking about buying a sailboat.

Celeste's mother would never allow him to do that, but Celeste could play along with his fantasy, and she managed to enjoy her afternoon with her father, despite her mind trying to insert Brad into everything, from how much he'd like the fish and chips to how he'd probably come to the sorbet shack every day until he tried all the flavors.

THE FOLLOWING DAY, CELESTE WIGGLED HER WAY INTO HER two-piece swimming suit, glad she'd gone for the bedazzled bikini. She could sparkle in the sun, and her dark shades would allow her to watch men without them knowing. Or families. Or couples. Anyone.

She packed snacks in her bag and put in a couple of bottles of water, slid in a can of sunscreen as well as her e-reader. She didn't feel like losing herself in a romance novel, but she was planning to spend the day on the sand, and who knew what afternoon would bring.

She arrived on the beach about the same time she

usually showed up for work, and Paige already had their spot staked out. "You got an umbrella," Celeste said as she set her bag on the ground beside the chaise.

"I know how weekends are on this beach," Paige said. "And I've had two guys stop by already."

"It's barely ten."

"They apparently play beach volleyball here on Sunday mornings." She waggled her fingers at the group of men a dozen yards away.

"Paige," Celeste whispered. "Those are *boys*, not men."

"Oh, they're legal," Paige said. "They're in college."

"Too young for my blood," Celeste said, suddenly feeling all thirty-seven of her years.

"I'm barely thirty," Paige said. "And that one is really cute." She giggled. "His name is Jack, and he's already put in our drink order."

"Virgin for me, right?" Celeste asked, though she knew Paige would've gotten it right. Her assistant was *very* good at her job, and Celeste turned toward her friend. "Never mind. Of course you got my drink order right." She reached over and took Paige's hand. "Thank you for being an amazing friend and an awesome assistant."

She didn't vocalize her appreciation enough, she knew that. Still, Paige's surprised look made a pin push into her heart. She needed to do a better job of letting the people around her know how much she appreciated them.

"Oh, my gosh," Paige said. "Did you get my text?"

Celeste frowned and pulled her phone out of her beach bag. "No."

Paige looked at her phone too. "It didn't send. I must not have noticed, because...."

"You were flirting with Mr. Muscles over there." Celeste could appreciate the volleyball skills of the boys in front of her. They all seemed to have the perfect tan, and the one Paige kept ogling definitely spent time in the gym.

Her phone beeped, and a link came up to The Island News. Celeste's blood ran cold. "I'm not reading that rag."

"This is a good story," Paige said. She laughed as the volleyball came rolling toward her.

A moment later, Mr. Muscles arrived, and he asked, "You want to come play?"

"Totally," Paige said, and she allowed the bronzed boy to pull her to her feet. She wore a much skimpier bikini than Celeste, which a woman seven years younger than her could. "Read that," she said over her shoulder.

Alone, Celeste couldn't really distract herself from the link. She tapped it open to find the headline of *The Whole Story Behind Bradley Keith, As Told By the Man Himself.*

She wasn't sure what she was going to get in the article, but she couldn't help reading it, especially when the first sentence was *Let me start by saying I've lost the best thing in my life since the article published a couple of weeks ago —and that's Celeste Heartwood.*

Her pulse rippled like the water did under the breeze, but she couldn't stop reading.

17

She's one of the smartest, sexiest women I've ever met, and first impressions of people aren't always right.

Brad glanced up from the paper when Joey scratched against his back door. He got up and let the dog in, scooping the little fluffball up into his arms. "She printed the article, bud. Maybe you'll get to meet Celeste today."

He sat back down at the dining room table and continued reading, which took all of his concentration.

When we first met, yes, Celeste Heartwood was uptight and a bit bossy. But I had just asked her to do me a huge favor —be my fake fiancée—and a lesser woman would've laughed at me and left me to deal with my problem on my own.

But not Celeste.

She has a heart of gold, and as we spent more time together, I realized—and told my friend, which the original author of the original article did not report—that what I thought were negative qualities at first were actually a benefit to Celeste.

She manages every event at The Heartwood Inn, and as I interviewed a few of the people she's worked with this week, it became even clearer to me that her attention to detail and demand for perfection are absolutely necessary. Without them, she isn't her, and I've started to fall in love with that woman, her demands and all.

He sighed and looked up. Maybe Bella had helped him with the article, just to make sure it didn't come off as too accusatory or too defensive. Oh, and to make sure all the right words got put in the right places.

"This is about *Celeste,*" Bella had told him at least a dozen times. "*She's* going to read this, and what she thinks and feels is more important than clearing your name."

He'd agreed with his sister, and he'd made any changes she'd suggested.

I just want the right story out there, the article continued. *And it wasn't fully reported. So yes, Celeste and I had a fake engagement, but we'd already started talking about how to break up at an appropriate time so as to not hurt anyone so that we could then start a real relationship.*

I'm sure she had first impressions of me as well, as she once submitted a proposal to my construction firm that went unanswered. As I dug to find out where her proposal had gone, my secretary found it had been filed with another project and we'd never seen it.

Well, we have now, and had I seen this proposal during the terms of the grant, I would've approved it. So it is with great pride and hope that I announce today that Keith Construction will be partnering with The Heartwood Inn to build an amazing outdoor wedding hall that will improve the grounds and bring even more people to Carter's Cove.

I don't know what will happen with Celeste and me. I know at one time she mentioned getting married on the property her family has owned for generations. It's probably a fool's hope to think she could forgive me and consider me for the groom in that grand ceremony.

But I suppose I've always been a bit of a fool.

No matter what, I apologize to any I've hurt through this ruse and want the people of Carter's Cove to know that everyone makes mistakes. And when I do, I own up to them. I apologize to my friends and family, and I especially apologize to Celeste Heartwood and her family.

Brad flipped the paper over so he wouldn't read it again. He'd already gone through it four or five times, and Celeste still hadn't called. He'd resisted the urge to go to her, to call her or text her. He'd put the article out there. She'd see it eventually, and he could wait a little longer.

He waited all day Sunday and didn't hear from her. He had to walk through the VIP pool at the inn and sign final paperwork on Monday, and his pulse skipped over itself a dozen times during the three-hour ordeal.

With everything cleaned up and the pool being filled by someone on the grounds crew at Heartwood, Brad stood in the hall and looked toward Celeste's office.

"Haven't talked to her?" James asked. "I'm sorry what we talked about made it into the paper."

"It's a local island paper," Brad said. "Fifteen thousand people, and they'd be lucky if ten percent of them read The Island Weekly." His throat felt so dry. "And Donna has all the details for the condo we got out in Mount Vernon Hills."

He'd been thinking of staying out there too. Just to clear his head. Get some distance from Carter's Cove, from Celeste. Maybe if he wasn't on the island anymore, he couldn't think about her day and night.

"I know," James said. "She texted me. That's my next stop."

"Let me know when you're going to go," he said. "I think I'm going to come too."

"You are?" James looked at him with surprise. "Didn't you just get a dog?"

"The condo is pet-friendly," Brad said.

"Oh, so you've been planning to come." James wasn't asking, and Brad wasn't sure what he'd planned for. He hadn't planned for his incredibly emotional and vulnerable article to go unanswered.

Literally, no one had said *any*thing to him about the words he'd written. No one besides Bella and his mother, that was.

"I'm still undecided," he said.

"All right. Well, I have tomorrow off, and I'll be heading out there on Wednesday."

"All right." Brad watched James walk away, and he couldn't help looking back toward Celeste's office. In the end, he couldn't just walk away. If she hadn't read the article yet, he could show it to her. Surely she'd at least accept his apology, and they could part on good terms.

His soul wailed at the prospect of that, because Bella had assured him Celeste would forgive him and they could start their real relationship once the article published.

With his palms sweating, he walked down the hall toward her office. Every breath became hard to take, and he almost stopped a couple of times.

The door opened, and he froze completely. "I'll just go back and grab it, Paige," Celeste said. "It's no problem. Has Gwen brought lunch?" He caught a glimpse of her before she headed back into her office. She continued to talk, but Brad's ears had filled with a white noise.

She was leaving, and he felt his only chance for closure slipping away. He opened the door and went inside the office, calling, "Celeste?" so she wouldn't be startled by him.

He didn't hear her heels clicking against the industrial carpet, but she suddenly appeared in the doorway. He hadn't heard her, because she wasn't wearing heels. Or shoes at all.

Instead, she wore a black bikini with a gauzy, white cover up that he could see right through. He forgot how to speak, and all he could do was drink in the tanned, toned sight of her, her messy, blonde curls spilling over her shoulders, and those beautiful, beautiful eyes.

"I can't let go of you," he said, unsure of where the words had come from. "I'm miserable without you, and I —did you see The Island Weekly yesterday?"

Celeste opened her mouth and said something he couldn't hear. She cleared her throat and said in a louder, clearer voice, "Yes, I saw it."

Brad just started nodding, pain spiraling through his whole body. "Okay." He exhaled and then scoffed. "Wow, that hurts more than I thought it would." He backed up, his fingers fumbling for the doorknob. "Sorry to bother you." He needed to get out of there, fast, before this woman cut his heart from his chest and squeezed it to shreds.

"I expected you to call," she said as he entered the hallway. "Maybe you've been off the island?"

"Why would I call?" he asked, not turning back. "I wrote the article. The ball is in your court."

"I texted you. I asked you to meet me at Redfin." She shook her head, her chin wobbling. Brad wanted to run to her. He'd have been anywhere she said—if he'd gotten those texts. "You didn't come, and I ate by myself."

"No." He moved back into the office. "I didn't get a text from you." He crossed the room to her, that bikini so sexy he could barely think. "Look. Take my phone." He handed it to her, and she did examine it, glancing up at him every few seconds.

"It appears that none of my texts went through." She stretched his phone toward him, and along with it, gave him hers. "Read mine."

Brad held her gaze before looking down at her phone. *Just saw the article.*

Meet me for dinner at Redfin at six? I'll have a private table in the corner.

Maybe you're not on the island. Traveling? I know you're transitioning between construction jobs.

That was it. She'd thrown the ball back, and he hadn't received the pass.

"I would've been there," he said. "At six last night, I had literally locked myself inside my house so I wouldn't drive around the island to find you." He gave her phone back to her, letting his fingers linger on her. "Every word was true."

"You're funding the outdoor wedding hall?"

"Of course. It's a brilliant proposal." He grinned at her, hating this fragile ground they were on. "But Celeste, the article wasn't about the wedding hall."

"I know." She nodded and tucked her hair behind her ear. She wasn't wearing makeup, and the scent of sunscreen hovered around her.

"I'm falling for you," he said. "And if you'll let me take you to dinner tonight, we can maybe see if we can make our fake relationship into a real one." He couldn't help smiling again, because he felt so close to getting her back.

"I know I can fall all the way in love with you if you'll let me."

There. He'd finally got all the words out that he needed to.

A tear slid down Celeste's cheek, and she swiped it away quickly. She smiled through the emotion, and she was so beautiful. "I'm falling for you too. Want to hang out with me, Paige, and Gwen on the beach today?"

Relief spread through Brad, and he chuckled. "Can I bring my dog?"

"You got a dog?"

He shrugged. "I've been really lonely, Celeste. When I lost you...." He shook his head and looked at the ground.

"Our beach is dog-friendly," she said. "Now get over here and kiss me."

Brad didn't need to be invited twice. He swooped Celeste into his arms, the feel of her absolutely perfect.

"I missed you so much," she whispered just before he captured her mouth with his.

18

Brad pulled up the inn, the early hour of the morning cool enough to make him smile. Of course, soon enough, it would be boiling hot, with the humidity supposed to be off the charts today.

He got out of his truck and started unloading the lumber he'd picked up the previous evening. He hadn't gone to Mount Vernon Hills, and he didn't have a a crew with him at The Heartwood Inn.

No, he wanted to build every inch of the outdoor wedding hall for Celeste—and then ask her to marry him in it.

Their new relationship was only a couple of weeks old, but it was going well. He'd only had to take a couple of steps back after the apology, and they'd been moving forward at full steam since.

In fact, he'd be seeing her for lunch that day, as it was

Tuesday, one of her lightest days for events at the inn. That was why both the bakery and their on-site restaurant had coupons for kids to eat free before six p.m.

He whistled while he worked, using his muscles for something besides running on the beach feeling really nice.

The excavator would be coming later that week to dig the hole for the building, and he had the cement trucks coming to pour the foundation early next week. Then Brad would be back with a hammer and nails and he'd get this hall built.

It wasn't that complicated of a project—it was just big. And Celeste deserved the best, so Brad would be making sure every piece of shiplap was lined up exactly right, so she could provide the ultimate wedding experience for her brides.

He finished unloading and he took a picture of the build site. He was planning to document it every step of the way and present a book to Celeste once it was finished. She'd commented on the old lighthouse they'd toured together last week that she liked the old photos on the wall showing the progression of the place.

Brad checked to make sure his football was still in the backseat of his truck, and then he drove through his nephew's favorite hamburger joint before heading to his sister's house. Celeste sat out front in her car, and Brad couldn't help smiling just from seeing her.

He parked in the driveway, and met her on the front

sidewalk. "Hey, gorgeous," he said. "How long have you been waiting?"

"Only a few minutes."

"You've met Bella. You didn't need to wait out here." He chuckled at the nervous look on her face. "She doesn't bite. Very hard."

That got Celeste to laugh, but it was short-lived, and she glanced toward the front door again.

"Here," he said. "You take the food. Tommy and Lizzie will love you then."

"I don't know why I'm so nervous to meet them."

"Yeah, why are you?" he asked, taking advantage of the sober moment. "You like kids, right?"

"I don't have a lot of experience with kids," she said. "None of my sisters have children, and yeah."

"Did you babysit when you were younger?"

"Yeah, that's why me an Gwen are so close. Olympia always had a date, and my mother favored her, so...."

Brad was still learning about all the complex relationship of Celeste and her sisters, particularly Olympia, so he just put his arm around her, handed her the bag, and said, "Let's go meet the troops."

He stepped in front of her once they got to the door, and he rang the doorbell three or four times before just walking right in.

Bella was yelling, and Tommy came skidding into the living room from the kitchen at the back of the house. "Uncle Brad!"

Brad laughed and lifted his nephew right off the ground. "Remember I said I was bringing my girlfriend today?" He looked at Celeste, because he'd never actually said the word girlfriend out loud to her.

She beamed at him, her eyes all melty-soft, and Brad knew he'd used the right term. "She's got your food, bud." He put Tommy down, who immediately moved over to Celeste.

"I'm Thomas," he said.

"Nice to meet you," Celeste said, and she sounded pretty stuffy in that moment. She lifted her eyes to Brad's. "I'm doing it, aren't I?"

"A little," Brad said with a smile. "She's Celeste," he added. "And where's Lizzie."

"That would be time-out," Bella said, arriving in the living room with a sigh. "She needs another couple of minutes. Hey." She leaned into Brad, who gave her a sideways hug.

"You remember Celeste."

"Of course." She smiled at Celeste and added, "Thanks for taking them today. I'm so ready for Greg to come home."

"How much longer?" Celeste asked.

"Ninety-four days." Bella flashed a smile, picked up her purse, and said, "Don't eat all the ice cream, Bradley. I'll need some tonight."

"Hey, I never eat all the ice cream."

"Every time," Bella said.

"I'll make sure you have some left," Celeste said.

"Hey," Brad said again, looking between her and his sister. They both just looked at him, saying so much without words. "Fine," he said. "I won't eat all the ice cream."

Bella nodded. "I'm off." She walked out the front door, at which point Lizzie peeked around the corner.

"Can I come out of time-out, Uncle Brad?"

"Yep," he said. "Tommy has the food. Let's eat it outside or in the kitchen. Take your pick."

"Kitchen," Tommy said. "It's too hot outside."

"Even for swimming?" Brad asked.

"Can we go to the water park?" Lizzie asked.

"The pool's not good enough?"

"It's boring," Tommy said.

"Wow." Brad chuckled as he followed the kids into the kitchen.

"Where does she go?" Celeste asked as Brad started to help Tommy unpack the burgers and fries.

"Who? Bella?" Brad glanced at her, handing her a chicken sandwich. "I have no idea."

"You don't ask?"

"Nope. Wherever she needs to in order to get her sanity back. Then she comes back."

"Are we sleeping over tonight?" Lizzie asked.

"Yep," Brad said. "Your mom said you'd have your bags packed. I think we know how that goes when I try to help."

By the look on Lizzie's face, she had not packed her bag before her mom left.

"That's why she was in time-out," Tommy said just before taking a big bite of his cheeseburger.

"I forgot pajamas last time," Brad said.

"For a sleepover?" Celeste asked. "That's like, the first thing you pack."

"Maybe you should do it." He looked at Celeste, and everything inside him lit up from the inside. "Go on, Lizzie. Take Celeste to your room and have her help you pack. Then we can go to the waterpark after lunch."

He'd told Celeste they might go swimming. Or to the beach. Or the waterpark. So he knew she'd have everything she needed to do that. She held his gaze for a couple of long moments, and then she smiled, and she was oh-so-sexy.

"I like the beach better," she said. "Have you guys ever been to the beach?"

"Yeah, sure," Lizzie said, dipping her French fry in a puddle of ketchup. "But Mom won't take us to the nice beach."

"The nice beach?" Celeste sat down at the table with the kids, no one making a move to go pack an overnight bag. Brad gave in and sat down as well.

"Yeah, the one over by the place with all the pools."

Celeste looked at Brad, and he just shrugged. "I own that place," Celeste said. "We can go there today if you want."

"Yeah, sure," Lizzie said, looking up at Celeste. "Do we have enough money?"

"Yes," Celeste said. "We have enough money."

"Celeste doesn't need money to go to that beach," Brad said, watching her. "Her family owns it."

"Your family owns the nice beach?" Tommy looked at her. "That's amazing."

"Right?" Brad asked. "So when we go, we have to be really good, or she won't let us come anymore."

"Criss-cross heart's promise," Lizzie said, her high-pitched girly voice making Brad laugh.

"And you have to pack your own bag," Brad said. "Or you're not coming."

His niece looked at him with alarm, and shoved half of her hamburger in her mouth. He shook his head and chuckled again, his threat totally without merit. He wouldn't leave Lizzie here, and she probably knew it.

Still, she did go down the hall to pack her bag, and Celeste went with her. They put their bags in Brad's truck and headed to "the nice beach" for the afternoon.

19

Celeste sure liked watching Brad throw a football to his nephew on the beach. The man had muscles *every*where, and with his shirt off...it certainly was very hot at the beach that afternoon.

Thankfully, she could watch him while wearing sunglasses, so it wasn't too terribly creepy. She applauded as his six-year-old nephew caught the ball, and then she glanced over to the sandcastle Lizzie had been working on for a long time.

She could learn a lot about a man as he interacted with kids, and Brad was fun, and kind, and patient. She knew nieces and nephews weren't the same as one's own children, but she sure did like the way Brad dealt with Tommy and Lizzie.

He eventually came back to the lounger she'd secured

for him, and Tommy sat down on the towel beside him. "I'm hungry, Uncle Brad."

"I'll order from the kitchen," Celeste said. "We have amazing nachos."

"Nachos?" Brad asked, and Tommy looked like he'd just been told he'd get Christmas twice this year.

Celeste laughed and started tapping on her phone. Gwen might not like Teagan, but the man made Celeste whatever she wanted whenever she texted him. She hadn't told Gwen that yet, but there was little her sister didn't already know, especially if it happened in the kitchen at The Heartwood Inn.

And a big salad, she added to her text. "Lizzie, are nachos okay for you?"

"Yep," she said.

"Brad?" Celeste asked.

"Will he make me a ham sandwich?"

"Of course."

And a ham sandwich. She sent the text, and put her phone in her lap. She'd worn a different swimming suit today, as Brad had already seen the black, bedazzled two-piece. Her white one-piece with the V-neck that went down to her belly button was still pretty impressive, and Brad had pulled her close as soon as she'd come out of the inn and said, "You take my breath away."

The feeling was mutual, and Celeste couldn't believe that she'd managed to take their fake relationship to a real one, even if the road had been a little rocky.

The food came in record time, and Celeste sent Teagan a big tip and a quick *thank you* text before returning her attention to Brad and the kids.

She watched him, her mind churning down a road it probably shouldn't even be on. He was a decade older than her, and she didn't have a whole lot of childbearing years left.

"Brad?" she asked as Tommy wiped his hands on a napkin.

"Hmm?"

"Never mind," she said quickly. They'd only been back together for a couple of weeks, and it was too soon to ask him about marriage.

"I'm going down to the water," Tommy said.

"Stay close," Brad said.

"I'm going with him," Lizzie said.

"You don't go in water deeper than your waist," Brad said. "I mean it."

"Okay." The little girl slipped away, leaving Celeste with no reason not to have a serious talk with him.

"What were you going to say?" Brad asked, reaching over and lacing his fingers through hers.

"It's...I was thinking about us," she said.

"Good things?"

"Good things." She glanced at him, the weight of his gaze on the side of her face too heavy for her to continue to ignore. "Marriage things."

"Oh-ho." He grinned at her. "What kind of marriage things?"

"I just was wondering...I mean, I'm only thirty-seven, but that's not a lot of years to have kids."

Brad just blinked at her.

"You know nothing about women, do you?" She laughed and swatted at his shoulder. He barely moved, because he was chiseled from rock and used to play professional football. Men his same size could barely move him.

He laughed and got up, crowding into her lounger with her. She let him, though there definitely wasn't enough room for both of them. She settled against his side, his arm around her comforting and warm and making her tingle from the soles of her feet to the top of her head.

"I've thought about marriage," he said. "But we don't need to rush, necessarily."

"What would be a rush?"

"I was hoping for a spring wedding in that outdoor wedding hall."

Celeste tilted her head back and looked at him. "Will it be finished by then?"

"How long do you think it takes to build something?"

"I have no idea."

"Well, I am the only crew member, so it is going to go pretty slow. But spring is like, nine months away."

Celeste focused back on the waves rolling in toward

shore, where Tommy and Lizzy played in the surf. "I suppose nine months is long enough to plan a wedding."

"Wait a second," Brad said, "I haven't asked you to marry me yet." His muscles tensed, which meant he didn't want to ask her to marry him right now. And frankly, Celeste was fine with that. She'd really only known him for a month.

But maybe their romance was written in the stars, and she didn't need more time than that. She kept all of her thoughts under her tongue though, because Brad still seemed like he was having a hard time breathing.

"I should probably know your favorite color before we get engaged," he said.

Celeste half-scoffed and half-laughed, the giggles winning as she started laughing fully. "I'm surprised you don't know."

"How would I know?"

"I wear this color more than any other."

"Navy blue."

She snuggled further into him, because he'd gotten it right. Brad was very observant about what she wore, and Celeste liked that. "You got it, quarterback."

"I didn't play quarterback," he said.

"I know." Celeste lifted his hand to her lips. "You played tight end, who is kind of like a receiver and kind of like a linebacker. You have to be fast, and strong, and amazing to play tight end."

"Did you look that up online?" he asked.

She had, and she looked up at him again, smiling. "I'm a little uptight sometimes."

"You are not," he said, looking down at her with perfect soberness. "You're wonderful, and smart, and beautiful, and talented, and organized, and you look amazing in navy blue pencil skirts, and white swimming suits." His voice dropped to a whisper by the time he finished speaking.

Celeste grinned at him, feeling warm and like he really felt and believed everything he'd just said. "I'm falling in love with you," she said.

"And I you." He matched his mouth to hers, and the bossy, uptight Celeste would never have allowed a kiss in public like this. So maybe she really was who Brad said she was.

"Can you send a magic text and get ice cream out here?" he murmured against her lips. And she could—but first, she wanted to kiss him again. So she did that.

A month passed, and the outdoor wedding hall took shape. Walls went up, and Celeste watched the progress of it from her second-story window. She saw Brad all the time, obviously, but he didn't talk much about the construction of it.

He worked a lot, managing his other sites and working

on the wedding arena, and she ended up taking his dog full-time. Joey was a sweet dog, but Celeste didn't exercise him as much as Brad had, and he'd taken to chewing some of Celeste's most prized possessions—her shoes.

She'd just wrestled one of her pale pink wedges from the dog's mouth when the doorbell rang. Frustrated and sweaty, she wiped her hair out of her face as she turned toward the door. She said nothing, because Brad would just come in, hopefully with a bag full of dinner.

Sure enough, he did, and he paused in the doorway. "He did it again." He wasn't asking this time, and his eyes dropped to the shoe she held in her hand. "Joey," he said. "You've got to leave her shoes alone." He closed the door, bringing the wonderful smell of fried chicken with him. "I'm sorry, sweetheart. I'll pay you back for those."

"It's fine," she said, tossing the shoe toward the box where she kept the dog toys. It was mostly full of shoes at this point, and she couldn't be mad all the time. "It's a shoe. Tell me that's from Jack-Jack's."

"It is, and I got the brown gravy and the peppered gravy." He smiled at her. "I'm really sorry about Joey. Should I take him back to the shelter?"

"No way," Celeste said, bending to pat the mutt. "He just needs some obedience classes. Sit. Sit." She pointed to the ground and straightened, and the dog sat. "See?"

Brad grinned and moved into the kitchen. "Let's eat. I'm starving."

"I'll bet. You started the day out in Mount Vernon Hills, right?" She followed him, glad when he took her into his arms and kissed her.

"Gross," Gwen said, looking up from her coffee mug. "If there's not a crispy chicken potato bowl in there for me, you're never allowed in this house again."

Brad stepped over to the bag and pulled out Gwen's dinner. "For you, Gwenny."

"I can't believe I let you call me that."

"You like it," Brad said. "How are things in the kitchen?"

Gwen tossed a look at Celeste, who also wanted to know the answer to that question. Her sister was going through a tough patch with men right now, especially Teagan.

"Hot," Gwen said with a smile.

"Is that a good hot or a bad hot?"

"It's just hot." She sat down at the kitchen table and took the lid off her bowl.

"Before we eat, I have a question," Brad said.

Celeste pulled her fried chicken box out of the bag and glanced at him.

He'd fallen to both knees.

"Oh, my goodness," she said, her words made of all air.

"Here it comes," Gwen said, delighted.

"Celeste," Brad said. "I'm in love with you. I know I've never said it out loud, but I've been feeling it more and more lately. I love you. I want to marry you in that outdoor wedding hall, and have a family with you, and take our kids to the nice beach every afternoon."

Celeste started weeping, though she'd told herself a dozen times she wouldn't. But she'd never been proposed to before, and he was so good, and so handsome, and so charming.

"Will you marry me?" he asked, reaching to open a drawer. A drawer right there in her kitchen.

"How long has that been there?" she asked as he pulled a black velvet ring box out of the drawer where she and Gwen kept their large kitchen utensils. "You kept a diamond ring with spatulas?"

"He's asking you to marry him," Gwen said. "Stop criticizing how he's doing it."

"I'm not criticizing how he's doing it."

"You haven't answered," Brad said, drawing her attention back to him. He opened the box to show a different ring than the one she'd worn previously. It was still huge, and still beautiful.

"Yes," she said, reaching to cradle his face in both of her hands. "Yes, I'll marry you."

He grinned and swooped her into his arms, laughing as he twirled her around. "Great. Is eight months long enough to plan the wedding?"

"More than enough," she said, looking right into those gorgeous eyes. "And I love you too, Bradley Keith."

She kissed him then—her very real fiancé.

Read on for a sneak peek at the next book in the series,
THE HEARTWOOD CHEF to meet the last Heartwood
sister and the man she definitely does NOT want...

SNEAK PEEK! THE HEARTWOOD CHEF
CHAPTER ONE

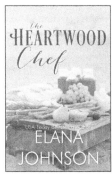

Gwen Heartwood paused just inside the doorway, the temperature in the kitchen almost hotter than outside. But that wasn't why she'd stopped out of sight. No, that was so she could take a long, deep breath of the scented air.

It always smelled a little bit like Teagan's cologne in the morning, before everyone else arrived and before the true cooking began. He beat her to work almost everyday, and she'd given up trying to be the first one in the kitchens at The Heartwood Inn. As far as anyone else knew, she was first and he second, as they all arrived after the two of them anyway.

Gwent tried to push the maddening man out of her mind as she rounded the corner and went into her office.

He didn't have one of those, and until a few months ago, they'd actually shared.

Shared a lot of things, actually.

A pang of sadness hit her, but she straightened her shoulders and pushed it away. *Not today*, she told herself. September had arrived, and it was time to get over Teagan Hatch. The end. Nothing more to it.

And for the first time in many weeks, Gwen actually thought she could do it. Her phone brightened with a text, but she ignored it. She knew who it would be from, and she wasn't in the mood to converse with her sister quite yet.

She sighed as she scooped her hair up into a ponytail. She had a lot of pale blonde hair, but it was very fine, and her heart swooped as she realized how tiny of a ponytail she made. Celeste had gorgeous hair, but she hated how she had to baby it so much. Gwen had learned over the years that everyone hated their hair. Women with curly hair wanted it straight, and those with straight hair wanted it to curl.

So she wished she had more hair than she did, while one of her best friends hated how thick her hair was— especially in the summer.

Gwen looped the ponytail up again and secured it a second time to keep her hair out of the way for the day. She donned her white chef's jacket, though she really just wanted to wear her T-shirt with a cartoon crab on the front.

But Teagan would be in his jacket, and by the way the air was now scented with onions and bacon, he'd already started the frittatas for their brunch buffet that morning. The hotel hosted dozens of conferences each year, and this breakfast buffet was for a small group of technology influencers staying at the hotel until Sunday.

She loved coming to work in the restaurant, but she sat down at her desk and pulled the schedule in front of her, so she'd look busy if someone came in. No one would. Everyone in the main kitchen knew exactly what time to arrive and exactly what to do once they did.

The outside door opened with its loud squeal, signaling the arrival of someone else. Gwen didn't need to guess who it was. Gage Sanders had taken over as the head pastry chef about six weeks ago, and he almost beat Gwen to work some days.

He claimed it was because he didn't sleep well, and Gwen was an early-riser too. Her sister, Sheryl, who was Gage's girlfriend, was not. Neither was Celeste, and Gwen wished she could stay home until ten o'clock in the morning.

Out of all the sisters, only Olympia worked more than Gwen did, and honestly, she was tired.

Only thirty years old, and tired already. Alone, and tired.

The adjectives were only getting more negative, and Gwen derailed her train of thought before she started spiraling again.

Besides, she had a new prospect for a boyfriend. Celeste had hosted a Love to Forty tennis event for singles at the inn a few weeks ago, and Gwen had gone. She'd met a few men there, and she'd been going out with anyone who asked. One man had asked a few times, and Gwen didn't entirely hate hanging out with Daniel Jenkins.

"He's certainly not Teagan," she muttered, immediately hating the words and wishing with everything in her that they weren't true.

Unable to distract herself with mindless administrative tasks, she got up and went into the kitchen. Gage worked at his station, his hands sure and his movements precise though he had no formal culinary training.

Gwen had gone to culinary school, but she could appreciate raw talent when she saw it. And Gage had it, as even the guests had started to notice the different bakery items his mind had come up with.

Gwen had worried about her sister's departure from the inn, but she now envied Alissa. Gwen didn't want to leave the family business. Not really. But she certainly needed a break. A vacation from her own life.

But she couldn't have one today. No, today, she was on the room service orders, and she stepped over to the stainless steel counter where she'd put together the items the delivery waitresses needed.

Scrambling eggs and pouring juice was easy work, and she loved the tiny little salt and pepper shakers, miniature bottles of ketchup, and the smell of bacon and sausage that came from her station.

Once she completed those orders, she'd attend a meeting with Teagan, as it was Friday, and he had a house special for Redfin every weekend. As the executive chef, it was his job to make sure everyone knew about the items from his sous chefs to the waitresses.

"Eggs Benedict," he called, and no one responded.

Gwen glanced around the kitchen, which had moved into its hot breakfast service for the bakery. Redfin, their on-site flagship restaurant, was only open for lunch and dinner, and Gage stocked all the baked goods in the bakery. But they also offered a short selection of hot items that Teagan made in between his other work, whether that be the catering or the meal prep for lunch and dinner.

Gwen stepped around her prep station and watched as Lilly, the petite brunette who'd put in the eggs Benedict order stood by the window, obviously trying to catch Teagan's eye. She was Gwen's opposite in every way, from the color of her hair to the curves she sported to how easily she could flirt with a man and walk away with a date.

Except for Teagan, obviously, as the man barely glanced at her. "We'll get it done, Lilly," he said.

She giggled, and Gwen rolled her eyes. "Do you need help?" she asked, trying not to focus on Teagan's gorgeous hair. The color of wet sand, his hair hung around his face, and he sometimes smoothed it back into a manbun that left every female who saw him swooning.

Gwen included, unfortunately.

"I'm not sure where Gordon went," Teagan said without looking at her. His voice took on a dead quality, almost a monotone. The same boring, and I'm-bored voice he'd been using with her in the kitchen since they'd broken up.

Gwen's pulse skipped over itself. "He went out on the floor," she said, nodding out the service window.

"Why would he do that?" Teagan's hands flew as he garnished a plate of pancakes with powdered sugar and set them in the window. Lilly didn't move to take the order out, instead still smiling at Teagan. "He's on the egg station this morning."

"I can do it," Gwen said. "And Lilly, you might as well give up. Teagan doesn't date."

Lilly's mouth rounded, she grabbed the plate of pancakes, and walked off. Satisfied, Gwen turned to the egg station. No, she hadn't made a poached egg for a while, but she certainly knew how. Her expensive New York City culinary education had taught her that much.

"I date," Teagan barked.

"You do?" Gwen laughed. "Since when?"

"You don't know what I do after I leave here," he said.

"Yes, I do," Gwen said. "Same as me. You drag your-self home after cooking for twelve hours and you collapse onto a couch somewhere, eating whatever you can find easily." She met his sea green eyes, almost daring him to contradict her. Or maybe she just wanted to swim around in those pretty eyes. She wasn't sure which.

He didn't argue with her, which meant she'd spoken true.

"You've been going out a lot lately," he said coolly.

Gwen blinked, because she wasn't sure what to do with what he'd said. He'd noticed? "Who have you been out with lately?" she asked, treading on very dangerous ground now. The last woman Teagan had been out with had earned herself a new stalker—at least for a few hours while Gwen searched and read everything the woman had ever posted on social media.

That hadn't ended well. In fact, Gwen distinctly remembered the stomachache she'd had after eating an entire carton of double chocolate fudge ice cream during the search.

She didn't mean her question to be a challenge, but Teagan's chin lifted, his way of saying, *Challenge accepted.*

Everything between the two of them was a challenge, and Gwen was tired of that too.

He didn't answer the question, instead saying, "Eggs Benedict," again.

"Yes, chef," she recited back to him, tearing her gaze from his. She hadn't asked him who he'd dated since her, but she already knew that answer: No one. In fact, in the five years Gwen had known the dark, mysterious, handsome Teagan Hatch, he'd only been out with the woman Gwen had looked up. Just her.

And then Gwen.

No one else.

As she poached the eggs, she couldn't help remembering those few months. They'd been amazing, filled with wonder and excitement as she learned more about the man who could put out a plate of delicious food better than anyone she'd ever met. She'd seen his soft side, and his funny side, and his adventurous side, and she'd liked them all.

Too bad he'd broken up with her out of the blue, with absolutely no explanation at all. And the man was a vault when he wanted to be. He could shut down faster than a convenience store at closing time, and Gwen hadn't been able to crack his stoic exterior since.

Her only comfort was that no one else had either—not even the giggly, voluptuous Lilly. In her chef's jacket, Gwen looked more like a man than a woman, which had become a reason to keep her hair as long as possible. Oh, and she wore oversized earrings everyday too. That helped her feel and look more feminine.

"Eggs Benedict," she said, placing the dish in the window, her body getting dangerously close to Teagan's.

He cut a look at her out of the corner of his eye, and Gwen pulled in a breath and held it. Time slowed, and when it came roaring back to full speed, she stumbled.

"Whoa," she said, her head spinning. She grabbed

onto Teagan's arm, and unfortunately, he'd reached for her plate of eggs in the window.

The next thing she knew, they were both on the floor, covered in hollandaise sauce and runny egg yolks.

I can't wait to see what happens when Teagan and Gwen get themselves cleaned up! Get THE HEARTWOOD CHEF in paperback now.

BOOKS IN THE CARTER'S COVE ROMANCE SERIES

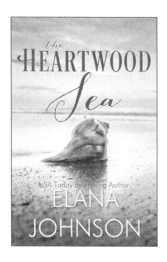

The Heartwood Sea (Book 1): She owns The Heartwood Inn. He needs the land the inn sits on to impress his boss. Neither one of them will give an inch. But will they give each other their hearts?

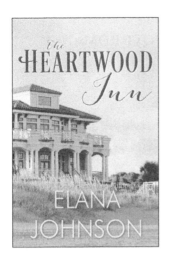

The Heartwood Inn (Book 2): She's excited to have a neighbor across the hall. He's got secrets he can never tell her. Will Olympia find a way to leave her past where it belongs so she can have a future with Chet?

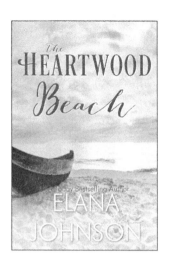

The Heartwood Beach (Book 3): She's got a stalker. He's got a loud bark. Can Sheryl tame her bodyguard into a boyfriend?

The Heartwood Wedding (Book 4): He needs a reason not to go out with a journalist. She'd like a guaranteed date for the summer. They don't get along, so keeping Brad in the not-her-real-fiancé category should be easy for Celeste. Totally easy.

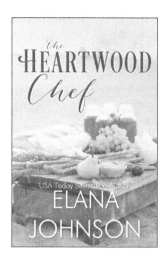

The Heartwood Chef (Book 5): They've been out before, and now they work in the same kitchen at The Heartwood Inn. Gwen isn't interested in getting anything filleted but fish, because Teagan's broken her heart before... Can Teagan and Gwen manage their professional relationship without letting feelings get in the way?

BOOKS IN THE HOPE ETERNAL RANCH
ROMANCE SERIES

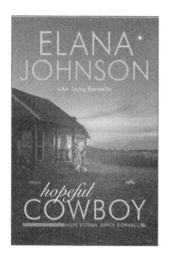

Hopeful Cowboy, Book 1: Can Ginger and Nate find their happily-ever-after, keep up their duties on the ranch, and build a family? Or will the risk be too great for them both?

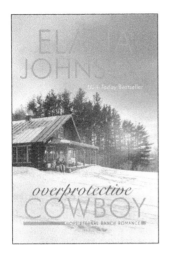

Overprotective Cowboy, Book 2: Can Ted and Emma face their pasts so they can truly be ready to step into the future together? Or will everything between them fall apart once the truth comes out?

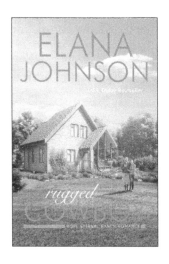

Rugged Cowboy, Book 3: He's a cowboy mechanic with two kids and an ex-wife on the run. She connects better to horses than humans. Can Dallas and Jess find their way to each other at Hope Eternal Ranch?

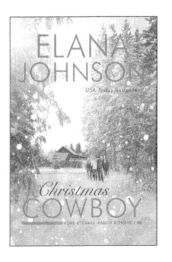

Christmas Cowboy, Book 4: He needs to start a new story for his life. She's dealing with a lot of family issues. This Christmas, can Slate and Jill find solace in each other at Hope Eternal Ranch?

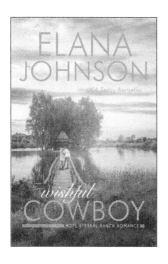

Wishful Cowboy, Book 5: He needs a place where he can thrive without his past haunting him. She's been waiting for the cowboy to return so she can confess her feelings. Can Luke and Hannah make their second chance into a forever love?

BOOKS IN THE HAWTHORNE HARBOR ROMANCE SERIES

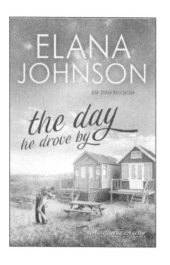

The Day He Drove By (Hawthorne Harbor Second Chance Romance, Book 1): A widowed florist, her ten-year-old daughter, and the paramedic who delivered the girl a decade earlier...

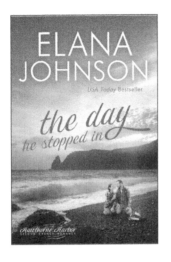

The Day He Stopped In (Hawthorne Harbor Second Chance Romance, Book 2): Janey Germaine is tired of entertaining tourists in Olympic National Park all day and trying to keep her twelve-year-old son occupied at night. When longtime friend and the Chief of Police, Adam Herrin, offers to take the boy on a ride-along one fall evening, Janey starts to see him in a different light. Do they have the courage to take their relationship out of the friend zone?

The Day He Said Hello (Hawthorne Harbor Second Chance Romance, Book 3): Bennett Patterson is content with his boring firefighting job and his big great dane...until he comes face-toface with his high school girlfriend, Jennie Zimmerman, who swore she'd never return to Hawthorne Harbor. Can they rekindle their old flame? Or will their opposite personalities keep them apart?

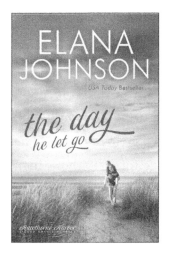

The Day He Let Go (Hawthorne Harbor Second Chance Romance, Book 4): Trent Baker is ready for another relationship, and he's hopeful he can find someone who wants him and to be a mother to his son. Lauren Michaels runs her own general contract company, and she's never thought she has a maternal bone in her body. But when she gets a second chance with the handsome K9 cop who blew her off when she first came to town, she can't say no... Can Trent and Lauren make their differences into strengths and build a family?

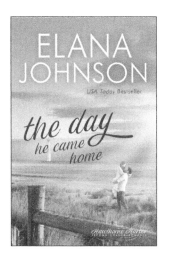

The Day He Came Home (Hawthorne Harbor Second Chance Romance, Book 5): A wounded Marine returns to Hawthorne Harbor years after the woman he was married to for exactly one week before she got an annulment...and then a baby nine months later. Can Hunter and Alice make a family out of past heartache?

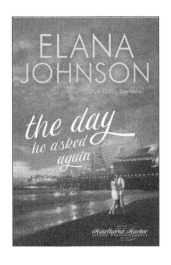

The Day He Asked Again (Hawthorne Harbor Second Chance Romance, Book 6): A Coast Guard captain would rather spend his time on the sea...unless he's with the woman he's been crushing on for months. Can Brooklynn and Dave make their second chance stick?

BOOKS IN THE GETAWAY BAY BILLIONAIRE ROMANCE SERIES

The Billionaire's Enemy (Book 1): A local island B&B owner hates the swanky high-rise hotel down the beach...but not the billionaire who owns it. Can she deal with strange summer weather, tourists, and falling in love?

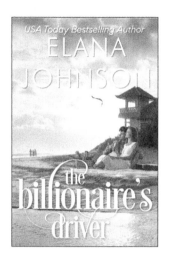

The Billionaire's Driver (Book 2): A car service owner who's been driving the billionaire pineapple plantation owner for years finally gives him a birthday gift that opens his eyes to see her, the woman who's literally been right in front of him all this time. Can he open his heart to the possibility of true love?

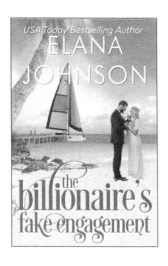

The Billionaire's Fake Engagement (Book 3): A former poker player turned beach bum billionaire needs a date to a hospital gala, so he asks the beach yoga instructor his dog can't seem to stay away from. At the event, they get "engaged" to deter her former boyfriend from pursuing her. Can he move his fake fiancée into a real relationship?

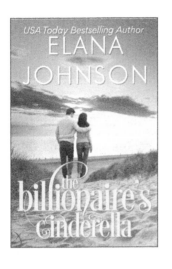

The Billionaire's Cinderella (Book 4): The owner of a beach-side drink stand has taken more bad advice from rich men than humanly possible, which requires her to take a second job cleaning the home of a billionaire and global diamond mine owner. Can she put aside her preconceptions about rich men and make a relationship with him work?

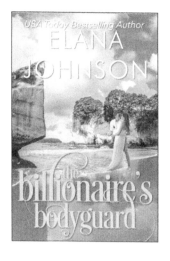

The Billionaire's Bodyguard (Book 5): Women can be rich too...and this female billionaire can usually take care of herself just fine, thank you very much. But she has no defense against her past...or the gorgeous man she hires to protect her from it. He's her bodyguard, not her boyfriend. Will she be able to keep those two B-words separate or will she take her second chance to get her tropical happily-ever-after?

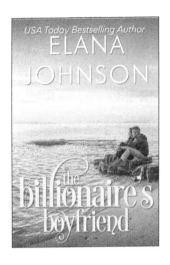

The Billionaire's Boyfriend (Book 6): Can a closet organizer fit herself into a single father's hectic life? Or will this female billionaire choose work over love...again?

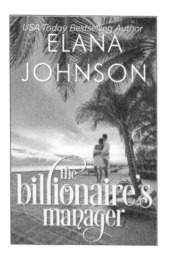

The Billionaire's Manager (Book 7): A billionaire who has a love affair with his job, his new bank manager, and how they bravely navigate the island of Getaway Bay...and their own ideas about each other.

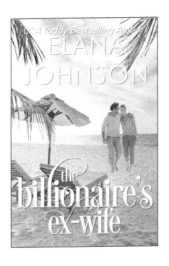

The Billionaire's Ex-Wife (Book 8): A silver fox, a dating app, and the mistaken identity that brings this billionaire faceto-face with his ex-wife...

BOOKS IN THE BRIDES & BEACHES ROMANCE SERIES

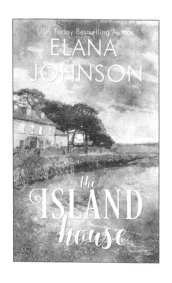

The Island House (Book 1): Charlotte Madsen's whole world came crashing down six months ago with the words, "I met someone else." Her marriage of eleven years dissolved, and she left one island on the east coast for the island of Getaway Bay. She was not expecting a tall, handsome man to be flat on his back under the kitchen sink when she arrives at the supposedly abandoned house. But former Air Force pilot, Dawson Dane, has a charming devil-may-care personality, and Charlotte could use some happiness in her life.

Can Charlotte navigate the healing process to find love again?

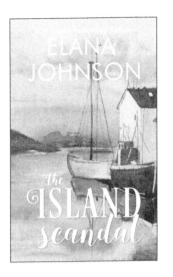

The Island Scandal (Book 2): Ashley Fox has known three things since age twelve: she was an excellent seamstress, what her wedding would look like, and that she'd never leave the island of Getaway Bay. Now, at age 35, he's been right about two of them, at least.

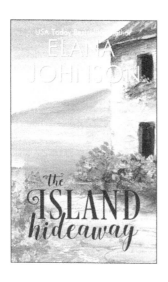

The Island Hideaway (Book 3): She's 37, single (except for the cat), and a synchronized swimmer looking to make some extra cash. Pathetic, right? She thinks so, and she's going to spend this summer housesitting a cliffside hideaway and coming up with a plan to turn her life around.

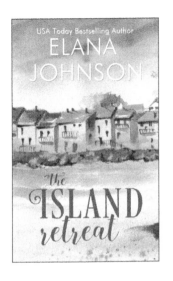

The Island Retreat (Book 4): Shannon's 35, divorced, and the highlight of her day is getting to the coffee shop before the morning rush. She tells herself that's fine, because she's got two cats and a past filled with emotional abuse. But she might be ready to heal so she can retreat into the arms of a man she's known for years...

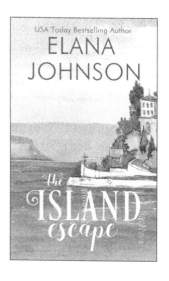

The Island Escape (Book 5): Riley Randall has spent eight years smiling at new brides, being excited for her friends as they find Mr. Right, and dating by a strict set of rules that she never breaks. But she might have to consider bending those rules ever so slightly if she wants an escape from the island...

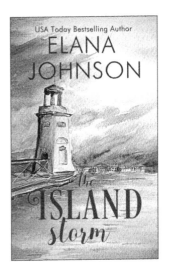

The Island Storm (Book 6): Lisa is 36, tired of the dating scene in Getaway Bay, and practically the only wedding planner at her company that hasn't found her own happy-ever-after. She's tried dating apps and blind dates...but could the company party put a man she's known for years into the spotlight?

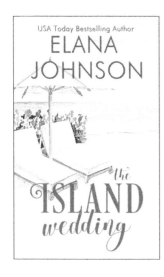

The Island Wedding (Book 7): Deirdre is almost 40, estranged from her teenaged daughter, and determined not to feel sorry for herself. She does the best she can with the cards life has dealt her and she's dreaming of another island wedding...but it certainly can't happen with the widowed Chief of Police.

BOOKS IN THE STRANDED IN GETAWAY BAY ROMANCE SERIES

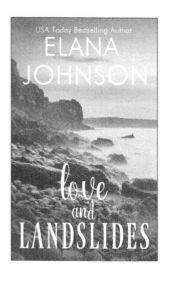

Love and Landslides (Book 1): A freak storm has her sliding down the mountain...right into the arms of her ex. As Eden and Holden spend time out in the wilds of Hawaii trying to survive, their old flame is rekindled. But with secrets and old feelings in the way, will Holden be able to take all the broken pieces of his life and put them back together in a way that makes sense? Or will he lose his heart and the reputation of his company because of a single landslide?

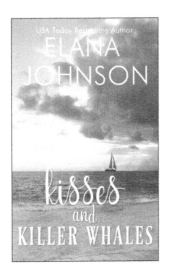

Kisses and Killer Whales (Book 2): Friends who ditch her. A pod of killer whales. A limping cruise ship. All reasons Iris finds herself stranded on an deserted island with the handsome Navy SEAL...

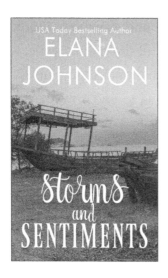

Storms and Sentiments (Book 3): He can throw a precision pass, but he's dead in the water in matters of the heart...

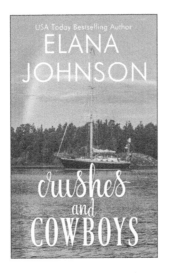

Crushes and Cowboys (Book 4): Tired of the dating scene, a cowboy billionaire puts up an Internet ad to find a woman to come out to a deserted island with him to see if they can make a love connection...

ABOUT ELANA

Elana Johnson is the USA Today bestselling author of dozens of clean and wholesome contemporary romance novels. She lives in Utah, where she mothers two fur babies, taxis her daughter to theater several times a week, and eats a lot of Ferrero Rocher while writing. Find her on her website at elanajohnson.com.

Made in the USA
Coppell, TX
09 November 2020

41042051R00146